My Spiritual Trail

My Spiritual Trail

By Robyn Heirtzler

Bonneville Publishers
Springville, Utah

ISBN 13: 978-1-55517-915-0
ISBN 10: 1-55517-915-0

Published by Bonneville Publishers, an imprint of Cedar Fort, Inc.
925 N. Main, Springville, UT, 84663
Distributed by Cedar Fort, Inc. www.cedarfort.com

LIBRARY OF CONGRESS CATALOGING-IN-PUBLICATION
DATA

Heirtzler, Robyn.
  My spiritual trail / by Robyn Heirtzler.
     p. cm.
  ISBN 1-55517-915-0 (pbk. : acid-free paper)
  I. Title.

  PS3608.E384M9 2006
  813'.6--dc22

                                                2006013691

Cover design by Nicole Williams
Cover design © 2006 by Lyle Mortimer
Printed in the United States of America

10 9 8 7 6 5 4 3 2 1

Printed on acid-free paper

DEDICATION

For my husband, who never gives up on me.

TABLE OF CONTENTS

TABLE OF CONTENTS

ACKNOWLEDGMENTS

I would like to acknowledge those who have had never-ending faith in me—my family and friends who saw my determination and helped me keep it. Thanks to Dave, Anita, and all the other writers who have encouraged me and given me advice.

I would also like to acknowledge the pioneers who gave up the comfort of their homes to travel across the country in search of peace and religious freedom. Their example is an inspiration to all and their hardships a true testament of faith.

Every time I pass the Market I think of her, every time I look in the river, I see her smile. And when I saw you rocking on the porch late last eve, I saw her so vividly I knew I could not face you.

—From the journals of Cateline Fortier

CHAPTER ONE

MOMMA'S TRUNK

March 5, 1862

I have cried what must be the last of my tears. At first I thought they would never stop. Now my eyes are red and my chest hurts, down deep like it did eleven years ago. I never thought I would feel better then either, but after a while I got better and the hurting stopped and left an empty place in my chest where the love used to be. Now it is filled with the hurt again, and I don't know what is better—emptiness or pain.

This must not make any sense at all since it is the first page in my book and I guess I really should explain a few things.

My name is Cateline Fortier. My mother was Maurine Fortier. She left me eleven years ago. I am now sure she is dead, though I don't like to think of it that way. I like to think that she is in heaven with angels and God, but I don't know much about those things. I have thought about her a lot. I know she wouldn't just leave me, so I know she must be dead. She loved me, and she was all I had. I was all *she* had.

She disappeared, and I never heard from her again and didn't know anything about her until I got this trunk. It doesn't tell me much, but it is a part of her and the things she had. I wish I could remember more about my momma and my life with her, but I was only four then, so my memories are poor. She used to leave me with Miss Anna, but that wasn't her real name. I don't remember her real name, but that is what I called her. My momma left me with Miss Anna while she worked, and one time she didn't come to get me. I knew something was wrong because she loved me, and I was so little and needed her bad. But she didn't come, and after a time they sent me here to live with Bart and Alva, who never called me Kate like Momma always did—just Cateline. I have worked hard here and learned to farm and hunt and shoot better than Bart can shoot and hunt. Alva taught me my letters and words and some cooking and sewing. They are good people and have cared for me.

Yesterday I was working with Bart in the fields,

and when we came in for supper it was just sitting there on the porch—a big trunk with my name on the top. I've never owned such a thing, and I looked at it carefully for the longest time until Bart dragged it in the house and said I should open it and see what it was. I did and that's when I cried. He saw me and went to the other side of the room and helped Alva cook, which is not a usual thing for him. Inside I found all of my momma's things: a fancy hairbrush and some ribbons, some books with their markers still in them, and this notebook. I held every little thing for a long time and rubbed the covers of the books with my fingers. The books are all leather, and I know they are old because they are cracked and faded. I found a letter from my momma's sister from only a couple of years ago in which she talked about her husband and her fine house and how she "regretted that her dearest sister Maurine would never know such happiness." I didn't know what she meant, and I read the date of the letter out loud many times because she wrote it nine years after I came to Bart and Alva. I read it again and was glad that someone saved it for me.

I found another letter in the trunk, folded with my name on the outside. "My Dearest Cateline," it said. I don't know anyone good enough for them to call me Dearest, and so I puzzled over it before I read any further. I have included it here so I would not lose it.

My Dearest Cateline,

    I only regret that I cannot return your mother to you. These are the last of her belongings, and I pray you will find some comfort in them.

    Every time I pass the market I think of her. Every time I look in the river, I see her smile. And when I saw you rocking on the porch late last eve, I saw her so vividly that I knew I could not face you.

That's all there was! No name or address or anything. I wondered why he would not come to see me and how he knew my mother so well. Did I really look like her? I don't remember her face or the way she sounded, but I wish I could talk to the man who does. After getting the trunk three days ago, I have not been able to stop thinking. I am not happy with my life here, and tonight I decided I will leave. I will look for my aunt and maybe then I can find out about my mother and who she was. The letter my aunt wrote sounded nice and friendly. She wrote about her big house, so she would have room for me if I could find her. I wonder what she will say when she learns of Momma. I wonder if she knows about me. She did not ask about me, but her life sounded busy with own her children and her *important* husband.

March 6, 1862

I have never done much with my hair, but today I sat on my bed and brushed it with my momma's brush. I brushed it until it was all shiny. I felt sad that she wasn't here to brush it for me or to tell me how pretty it was. I wonder if she had hair the same yellow as mine. I tried to picture her in my mind as I rolled my hair at the back of my head in a chignon. I pinned it in place and turned my head back and forth, smiling the way I thought she would do. Then I pulled it out and braided it like usual.

March 7, 1862

This trunk sure is a fancy thing. I wish I could take it with me when I leave, but it really would be too big for me to handle alone, and I don't have near enough belongings to fill the whole thing.

March 8, 1862

When we sat down to eat last night, Bart and Alva were quiet like always and got all in a pucker when I spoke. I told them my plans and about my aunt, who I thought would take me in until I could find some work. Alva nodded and whispered, "I'm sure she will." Bart just sat stiff and then grunted and frowned.

I told them I would stay until we had the field planted. Bart just nodded. He didn't even look at me, so I was quiet and ate until we were all done. Bart wiped his mouth and said, "She might not take you." I didn't know what to say, so I stayed quiet.

"She didn't take you after your mother was kilt. What makes you think she wants you now?" he asked.

I didn't know, but I had to go and find out, so I told him that maybe she didn't know about me. He shook his head and muttered, "Sakes alive, girl." He put on his hat and went out to finish chores. I watched him, but I didn't follow to help.

I have been here a long time, and I am ready to leave. When I first came, Alva was thin and pretty and Bart didn't have any of the grey that's in his hair now and his back wasn't bent so bad. He used to talk to me too; he used to smile and tell stories while we worked. They're old now and it's not just their bodies, their minds seem to be worn out.

May 15, 1862

I brushed my hair for some time tonight and then I put on my momma's fancy slippers and danced around my room like I was at some wedding party. I twirled around and thought about the boys who might want to dance with me and then I sat down. I know that if I don't leave here soon I will just get old and I will lose my smile like Alva.

April 2, 1862

I feel like I need to work hard to make up for leaving Bart and Alva without my help. I have been so tired in the evenings that I have not even been able to write about all I am doing. I will leave soon and I will have my own life and my own dreams.

April 10, 1862

I held my momma's books today and her ribbons and her letters. I wondered if I could take them all with me. I don't think I will be able to, so I have sorted through it all and picked out the things that remind me most of her. I have kept two books that look faded and worn like she read them a lot—one is called *Indiana* and it has something to do with Paris where my momma was from and the other is *Eclectic Readers*. I haven't looked at it really well yet to see what it's about. I reckon I'll read them both when I get settled at my aunt's. I have decided to keep Momma's brush and a few ribbons too.

There are other things like a gown that are too fancy for me to ever wear and I will leave that here in the trunk it came in. I will also leave the slippers—I could never wear them out of the house and they are small for my feet anyway. It hurts to leave anything but I know I can't take it all and I hope one day I can get the rest of it, wherever I end up.

April 15, 1862

I put a note in my trunk with my momma's things all folded nice and explained about the things that were in it. I asked whoever found the note to please send me the trunk and I wrote down my aunt's name and the city she lives in. I hope one day it will be sent, but I don't think Bart or Alva would ever do it. So I am leaving it up to a stranger to find me.

May 10, 1862

Alva pulled me aside today while we were hanging up the wash. She gave me a quick hug and I saw some tears in her eyes. She let go of me and went back to the clothes. I watched her for a while but she didn't act any different, just like it didn't happen. I wonder if she will miss me. I think that was the first hug I ever got from her. Maybe there are some feelings that she has never expressed to me before. I'm going to try and be extra nice before I leave.

May 20, 1862

I made supper today and it tasted really good. I told Alva thank you for everything, and she didn't say anything. It was uncomfortable for both of us, but I had to say it anyway.

May 23, 1862

I went hunting and got a fine deer. Bart skinned it and Alva helped me cut it up. It is in the smokehouse and I feel better to know it is there.

June 1, 1862

I am so nervous I can't sleep. Tomorrow I am leaving on the train. I've never been outside of town before. My heart beats faster every time I think of it, and I have to make myself be still and not run to the depot right away. Alva worked harder than normal today and Bart didn't say a word. He is taking me to the depot in the morning, and I only hope he is not angry that I am not going to be here during the harvest. He is a strange, quiet man and even after eleven years I can't understand him.

The candle by my bed is almost gone and I need to stop writing now and try to sleep.

June 2, 1862

I am on the train! It is not at all like I thought it would be. The wheels rattle terribly over the tracks, and the ashes from the smokestacks are sure thick over us.

I am traveling in what they call the ladies' car. It's

supposed to be for the ladies so they don't have to worry about men's company and such but I don't see that it's any better than any other car on this thing. The seats are hard and my back is sore even though it is still early. It is a new and exciting and scary time.

I waved to Bart when the train started to leave, but he did not see me. He had his back to the train and was getting in his wagon. I am now here with people I have never met, and my hands are shaking something terrible. I have a bag that Alva gave to me and it is full of goods that I might need on my way. I have my letter from my aunt so I can find her and the letter from the man who gave me the trunk. I also have some biscuits and jerky.

I wish my momma left some kind of book for me because I would like to know what she felt and what she saw, and I would like to know all about that place across the ocean where she was born. I would like to go there some day and see if I have any family there. Maybe Aunt Jolie can tell me some of these things.

I wonder about this place I am going, Fremont. I don't know anything about it and Bart had to ask someone where it was so we could buy a ticket there. It's only a few days away, and I am glad there is a train that goes all the way there.

June 3, 1862

I kept waking up last night and could not eat this morning. I don't know if I am sick from the train or if I am sick from being on my own. It is probably both.

June 4, 1862

Now I have to write a little about what they call a *refreshment saloon*. That is where the train stops, and we all get off to eat. This morning I was feeling much better and I was hungry because I didn't eat much yesterday. Well we got to one of those *refreshment saloons* and the conductor yelled, "Breakfast, fifteen minutes." I about yelled back that we had thirty minutes yesterday! But I didn't. I just hurried and ate so fast there that I think I made myself sick again. I hope we have more time for lunch or I may not keep it down.

I am glad this is my last day on the train.

A woman knocked on my door today and I asked her to come in. She did and sat in a wooden chair next to the door. I sat on my bed and asked her how I could help her. She said she had known the Walters family—which is the last name of my aunt.

—From the journals of Cateline Fortier

CHAPTER TWO
FREMONT

June 5, 1862

I wanted to search for my aunt right away, but when I got to the depot it was late and I was so tired. I knew it wouldn't be too good to show up late and disturb them with all their children, so I was glad when I saw a hotel runner. He told me about a fine place to stay and even carried my bag there for me, which was good because I didn't want to carry it myself. But I made it and it sure is a fine place, just like he said. I slept well but was so nervous this morning that I brushed my dress and took care with my hair! I think I am ready to meet my family, and I could cry because I am so happy.

June 6, 1862

Fremont is sure a lot bigger than the town I lived by before. The houses are all spread out a ways, and it took some time but I found out that I need to go south to find my aunt's house. It is too far to walk in a day and I think I have found a man with a shay that I can hire to take me there. I will take my bag with me so I will not have to come back here.

June 7, 1862

I have certainly gone and got myself in a fix now. I should be in a nice house with my family and talking about everything we have missed, but I don't know if that will ever happen now. Even with that driver who knows the place, it took some time to find the house I was looking for and when we stopped in front of the gate I got sick. I asked him was he sure this is where they lived and he said it had to be and shrugged his shoulders like the house was there last time he looked. Only now it wasn't there, nothing was there except for some ashes and burned wood. Even the trees that were there once have been cut down because now there are just big stumps. I went through the gate and walked around for a while. I even cussed out loud and then saw that the driver was right behind me. It serves him right for following me.

I don't know what to do now. I have a powerful pain in my chest again and this time my stomach too. It hurts so bad that I don't think I will ever be happy again.

Well that driver said he wouldn't charge me for the ride and I said thank you. He said it was all he could do but he wished it was more. I asked him if he knew the people who lived there, and he said no, but the barber might. I said I would ask the barber then and asked him to drop me there. We rode the rest of the way in quiet. The barber shop was closed when I got there and I will go in the morning to ask him. I hope they are alright and still live close so I can find them. I don't have a lot of money and I can't go on the train again, so I found a small room to rent until I can find my aunt.

June 8, 1862

I talked to the barber today, but he wasn't very friendly and only said that they stopped coming in some time ago and he didn't know what happened to them. He said that they had a few fine horses and the farrier might know something. I thanked him and left. Well, the farrier told me he was new to town, and he started shooing when the other man left to go west with the Mormons. Now I don't know what the

Mormons are and I really didn't care. He could see this, I think, and said he would ask around and that I should check with him in a couple of days. I told him I would. I hope I don't run out of money before then. It's now been days that I've been trying to find my aunt and her family and I am scared that they might have left me like my momma did.

June 10, 1862

I have decided I better look for work.

June 11, 1862

A woman knocked on my door today and I asked her to come in. She did and sat in a wooden chair next to the door. I sat on my bed and asked her how I could help her. She said she had known the Walters family—which is the last name of my aunt. I asked her if she knew where they were and she nodded but did not seem happy to tell me. I asked her if she would tell me where they were and she nodded again real slow. Then she told me their story. She said she was sorry and I couldn't speak and she got up and left.

She said that there were bad times in town a while back and Aunt Jolie got real sick. Her babies got sick too and they didn't make it. She missed them so bad she couldn't eat. The woman said nobody was real sure what happened, but she died only a couple weeks after her babies.

Her husband—my uncle—got mad and didn't want no reminders about his wife and children, who were all buried now, and he set fire to his fancy house. After it burned down he lived in an alley and spent all day drinking and cussing. She said it was all his loneliness that made him do it, and he was sure in a hurry to get to his family because he drank more than any man ought to and one morning he just didn't wake up from all the whiskey he'd been drinking. She said he was a good man though and didn't ever mean anybody any harm, but he couldn't live without his family. He had tried everything to forget them and to get all that had happened out of his head.

I am sorry for my uncle and I wish I could have known him. Maybe I could have helped him.

June 12, 1862

I went in my first bar today and talked to the barkeep. He seemed a bit surprised that I was in there but he talked easy and I asked him if he knew my uncle. He said he knew him. I asked if he knew how he died, and the barkeep told me the very same story so I know it is true. It didn't happen long ago either, only a couple of weeks. He said that my uncle didn't want to go on living and he wanted his family back so bad. He told everyone his story when he was drunk, the barkeep said, and they would always buy his whiskey for him.

It is a sad way to die, but I know how it feels to

be alone, and I won't be the one to judge him bad for what he's done.

June 13, 1862

I walked to the cemetery today. I found the graves of my family and I looked at them for a long time. I cleaned them off good because they were covered with dirt. I found my aunt Jolie's grave and there were three more of her children's. It sure is sad that they all died and I never even got to meet them. My uncle's grave was farther away and it was just a little board with his name on it. I wish I could move him closer to his family.

June 14, 1862

Nobody wants to hire a little girl to do their work. I will look again tomorrow.

June 15, 1862

Still nothing, and I wonder if I will have to starve in my little room. Such a strange place—I was out all day and all I saw was four wagons. They were different than any I've seen before and I stared until I walked right into a big man in front of me. He worked his jaw as he watched them and didn't seem to notice that I ran into him. I asked him where it was they were going and he shrugged his shoulders.

"They got a meeting place north of here," the man told me. "They're Mormons."

I asked him what he meant by Mormon. He stared at me hard then and spit in the street. I didn't like the way he looked at me and I went in a store and looked at yard goods until he was gone.

June 17, 1862

I worked today for an old woman who needed some help fixing fences. She didn't want to let me do it at first but I told her I lived on a farm my whole life and that I knew how to do hard work. She said she couldn't pay much but she would give me a try. I guess I did alright cause she paid me with stamps that she said could be used as money. She fed me good too, and it was worth it just for the food because I have not ate like that in a long time.

June 18, 1862

The lady was right about the stamps. I showed them to the man at the store and he told me what they were worth. I know I am being foolish to buy something other than food right now but it is so hot here that I got me a flat to wear while I am in the sun. The brim is wide enough that it shades me from the sun better than my bonnets do and it will be nice if I get to help that lady again.

I've never seen anybody with hair as bright as his and he was all tall and skinny and looked like wheat flopping in the wind the way he laughed.

—From the journals of Cateline Fortier

CHAPTER THREE
THE MORMONS

June 21, 1862

I met a Mormon man today. I was talking to the man at the dry goods store, trying to get work sweeping or cleaning because I know I would do good but he wouldn't talk to me. I asked him why he wouldn't hire me and he said he didn't need no help and besides he couldn't pay me. I said I didn't need much but he still wouldn't listen. I didn't know what to do then because I'm tired of talking to people and asking them for work. I decided to go back to that old lady's house and see if there was anything more I could do for her. When I was leaving the store, this Mormon man took off his hat and said hello. I nodded at him. He asked if I was looking for work, and I nodded again. He looked real thoughtful then, and I asked him if he knew where I could find some work. He shrugged and tipped his head and said he might know. I told him then that I never asked no odds and I did my fair share of work and did it good. He smiled a little and then he went to his shopping and said he would get back to me. He seems like an odd man to me, but nice enough. I really don't expect him to come back, but if he does I hope he comes quick because I only have enough money for a few more days at the room I've got and my stomach doesn't stop with its grumbling. I'm terrible hungry and I know I'm in a mess.

June 23, 1862

I have one night left in my room and not enough to buy my breakfast. There's no more work at that lady's house, Mrs. Kent, she said her name was. She did give me some biscuits and told me thank you again for what I done last time.

June 25, 1862

Last night I walked around town until I was so tired I would have slept in an alley, maybe even challenged a man to a gunfight and get myself shot so I wouldn't be so hungry. That is when I found an empty stable and clean straw to sleep on. I was grateful to have the roof above even if it was full of holes. I have no money for food and will try to find some of the wild berries like I used to pick at Bart and Alva's to eat this morning. I may just have to start walking back to Bart and Alva's house and see if I can find work on the way somewhere. But that is the very last thing I want to do.

Finally a bit of good news! While I was picking berries, the Mormon man came back and said his name was Brother Williams. He brought his friend, Brother White. Brother White is the one who needs someone to help him but he said he would not be able to pay me wages. Instead, he said he would give me food and a bedroll if I could travel with them to Salt Lake City. When we get to the city, he said there will be work for me and the people there would gladly take me in until I could get a place of my own. I asked him why they would help someone they didn't know and he said that's what God wants them to do.

I don't know anything about this Salt Lake City and I don't know much about the Mormons except that they must be some religious kind of people. He asked if I was willing and I asked him what the work was. He said his wife was quite ill and couldn't take care of his little ones. I told him I never cared for children before and he said they were good children. He said he needed somebody to cook and set up camp each night. It is a lot of work, he told me, but it will be worth if for you. I asked him about his children and his wife and he answered plainly. He said his wife could not get around and she was in bed most of the time. She can't do much of anything so I would have to do it all. I told him I was a hard worker and he nodded real little.

He asked if I had a family. I told him no. He wanted to know where my parents were. I said, "My mother is dead."

Then he asked about my father.

I said, "I ain't never had a father."

He raised his eyebrow when I said this and then he said I could still work for him if I wanted. I told him I would do it and he carried my bag to his wagon right then.

I got a hot meal that he cooked and I met his two children. I am glad that he will not do all the cooking. I am not a good cook but Brother White is worse. Still I am glad for the food and I told him that when we ate.

June 26, 1862

I met Ashley today, that is Brother White's wife. She is very thin and weak. Still, she is pretty and she has a soft voice that sounds like the south. I like her and I feel sorry that she can not take care of herself or her children. She said she was glad I came and that I was beautiful. I don't think she was looking at me very well when she said that, but still she said it and it made my heart thump in my chest. Nobody ever told me that before.

There are two little ones. Martha is four and

Samuel is one. He is still wobbly on his feet and his hair is real yellow and sticks up all over. Martha is thin as her mother but healthy and she doesn't say a word. I wonder if she doesn't know how to talk or if she is just scared like I was when I got on the train. I think she is probably scared because of her momma being sick and them leaving their home and living by this wagon all the time.

June 27, 1862

Martha watches me and follows me everywhere I go—but she won't talk to me. Samuel climbed in my lap today and played with my hair and made little baby noises that made me smile. I like these children and I hope I can take care of them well like Brother White says. I don't know his first name and I don't know why he wants me to call him brother.

June 28, 1862

I asked Brother White when we would leave and he said we were waiting for others to come. There are already maybe twenty wagons parked near us and I asked, "Why do we have to wait for more?"

He said, "There are others that will be coming from across the ocean, and we have to wait for them."

I asked, "How long?"

"A couple of weeks, maybe a month."

I told him that if we had to wait that long, then I

was going to go hunting so we could have some fresh meat, and he looked at me real funny. I asked could I borrow a gun because I didn't have a one.

"Do you know how to shoot it?" he asked.

"I could out-shoot you," I replied, and his mouth opened but he didn't say anything.

He pointed to a tree and said, "Show me."

When he gave me his rifle I asked which branch, and he looked at me sideways again.

"Just hit the tree," he said.

I shot the tree in the center. He grunted and nodded. I said I could shoot out the little branch on the side and he started to walk away.

I lifted the gun and shot quick. The little branch was gone and Brother White looked at me for the longest time. Then he said, "There are probably a few deer to the north because I saw their tracks. Sister White would appreciate some fresh broth." He led his good black horse to me and I jumped on and left.

Now I am sitting in the shade on a huge rock, around me there is grass and flowers like this little yellow one I will place in the folds of this book when I finish writing this page. I love the smell and the air here. If I was those Mormons, I think I would build my house right here instead of going to that Salt Lake City like they keep talking about.

July 1, 1862

From the way the Mormons reacted, you would think a woman never shot a deer before. Shooting it was easy, it was getting it back that took a little more time and I just tied it to the saddle horn and drug it back. I had lots of help when I got back to the wagon and some men even skinned it for me so I didn't have to do a thing but cook it later. These are nice people and I think I will like to travel with them.

Ashley is very sick and just sipped a little broth for her supper last night. I told her that if she didn't start eating good she wouldn't feel much better, and she told me real nice that it didn't matter what she ate. I tried to tell her that she needed the food for her strength and she just smiled soft at me. Her eyes are light green and so wide all the time but she does not look scared.

I took the children down to a small stream this morning, and they took off their shoes and kicked their feet in the water. They threw rocks in too, and Samuel laughed at some fish before he scared them away. I made a necklace out of grass for Martha and she smiled when I put it around her neck. I helped her make one to take back to her Momma.

July 4, 1862

There was quite a frolic today. All the Mormons came with pies and cakes and preserves. There were biscuits and sausage and fine things like I haven't seen since I got on the train. It was a great feast! There were games too—the children all played Run Sheep Run and Blindman's Bluff and so many other games that kept them laughing all day. There was a big dance in the night and I watched it from a ways off with the children. I put them to bed when it got time and then I laid down and listened to the music go on for a time. That's when I got up and built this fire and decided to write about it all. It sure is a sight and I kind of wish I could go on over there and some boy would ask me to dance.

July 5, 1862

More wagons came today and there must be close to thirty now. I wonder how many more there will be before we leave. I am not in a hurry, though, because I am fed and have a bed to sleep in. I have the little ones to keep me busy and the cooking and wash. Sometimes I sit by Ashley and talk to her or read to her from one of her books, but I have to stop sometimes and have her help me with the words. She has one she likes a lot and it has words I don't know so I read real slow and I don't understand any of it. But she likes it and says I do a fine job. Brother White has made a shelter for her and a nice bed for her to rest on. He sure looks like a rough man, but his heart is kind.

July 6, 1862

I was right about the Mormons being some kind of religious people. They say prayers over everything and they all call each other Brother and Sister even though I don't think any of them really are. They even have their own book, the *Book of Mormon*. This is the one I have trouble reading to Ashley but she likes it so I keep reading and sometimes I can even tell that there is a story there. Ashley said it's a record of the people on the American continent, but I'm not sure what she means. I told her that I have some books that used to be my momma's and she said she'd like to see them sometime. I think I will get them out and read them to her if she wants.

All the people are gone to church now and it is awful quiet. Ashley invited me to go with them but I shook my head like before and she didn't argue. She said that a body had a right to make up their own mind and that they would be back before long. I watched as Brother White carried her to their meeting and I ached a little inside but don't know why. I think it is because she is so weak.

July 9, 1862

Today a considerable number of people came with wagons. I think it is the ones we are waiting for. It is crowded now and I think we will leave soon, but I have not been told.

The little ones are well and happy. Samuel fell in the stream this morning and cried for about a hour, but Martha got him some dry clothes and I changed him and rocked him to sleep and now he is snoring softly. Ashley is resting. I made her some raspberry tea and she drank half a cup before she fell asleep. I think I will get some more leaves this afternoon so I can make her more.

July 10, 1862

I walked around our strange new town today. A town of wagons and beds on the ground, cook fires and people. I counted eighty-four wagons! I stopped to talk to a new family, but I couldn't understand them and they all just waved at me and smiled.

I started to walk away when somebody talked behind me. "They don't speak English," he said.

I turned to look at him and asked, "Do you?"

He laughed at me then and I frowned hard at him, but it didn't do no good. I've never seen anybody with hair as bright as his and he was all tall and skinny and looked like wheat flopping in the wind the way he laughed. I went to leave him and he stopped me and held out a hand. I looked at it but didn't touch it.

"My name's Colier Cranston," he told me. It was hard to understand him because he says his words all wrong.

"Hello," I said.

He smiled at that, but I didn't think it was funny.

"What's your name?" he asked.

I told him my name and said that my momma used to call me Kate. I don't know why I told him that, but he just said, "You're not French."

"No," I said, "but my momma was."

He asked, "Where is she?"

"I don't have a family no more," I answered.

He got quiet then and I told him I had to get back and help Brother White with his little ones. He walked with me partway, but I wouldn't look at him or talk to him, so he left when we got close and ran back to his wagon.

July 11, 1862

It sure is a mess here with so many people waiting to go someplace they've never been and don't know much about.

July 12, 1862

We leave soon. We are just waiting for the skandenaviens to get the rest of their supplies. That's what Brother White said they were, and I never heard the word before, but I did my best to write it out. He said that's why they don't speak English. I nodded, and he left to help one of the families.

I hope I am doing enough work that Brother White won't want to leave me behind. I have nothing here and nothing to go back to. Maybe my new life and dreams are in Salt Lake City with these Mormons.

There was a herd of buffalo today like I've never seen before and it like to scared me to death before I realized they would not hurt us. The whole earth seemed to be covered with them and they passed right in front of our wagons so that we had to stop and wait for them to get out of the way before we could go any further.

—From the journals of Cateline Fortier

CHAPTER FOUR

TRAIL LIFE

July 13, 1862

Colier came to Brother White's wagon today. He just walked right up with Brother White when he came back from his church meeting. He had an old woman with him and he told me it was his mother. I said hello to her and she smiled kind but sad. I knew the look because I felt it all the time in my chest. I sat outside the wagon and fed Martha and Samuel while Colier's mother went to see Ashley, and Colier stared at me and made jokes. He calls me Kate and I am mad that I told him that name. I don't know why he laughs so much, but it bothered me so I asked him why his mother came to see Ashley because she doesn't even know her. He shrugged his shoulders and said his mother knows a lot about sicknesses and healing and women. I didn't know what to say then, but I am glad she is here and hope she can make Ashley better.

July 14, 1862

Brother White has been working hard every day. He is sure good with that horse of his, and everyone else must have seen that too because now he is putting shoes on all kinds of horses and he rode the buck out of one while I watched. It would take a mean horse to get him off, and I wonder where he learned to do all that.

July 16, 1862

I wonder if it is possible to travel to Salt Lake City because we are only going a few miles a day. I have heard talk of how far we have to go and it makes me wonder if we will even get there this year. It took hours to get all the oxen hitched up and the wagons loaded this morning, and then they moved so slow that I walked with the children beside the wagon. I could have gone faster on my own. We stopped while it was still light out and made camp for the night. I feel like if I look hard enough I can even see the spot down the trail where we stayed before. But I can't see the wagon covers from the people who stayed behind and I know we have gone farther than it seems.

Ashley did fine today, and I think maybe this slow pace will be good for her. After supper I read to her for a while, and then Brother White carried her to a fire in the center of all the wagons—all the wagons make a big circle. The sun set, and the music started around the fire. Some people had harmonicas and some were singing. One old lady even beat spoons together to the music, and then people got up and danced. Some danced alone and others grabbed partners and danced with them. I saw that Colier boy and he was dancing with an old woman for a while, and then she turned and I could see it was his mother. He made her laugh too, but I couldn't hear what he said to her. Then I looked at Ashley. She had tears in her eyes and was looking at Brother White real hard like she was remembering a time long ago, and I had to leave.

She is so beautiful and she is young and her children are scared so I have a hard time when I see her look all sad like that. I know that Ashley will not see Salt Lake City. I don't know what is wrong with her or why she is sick, but she looks at Brother White and her children with a look of good-bye.

My own fire is dying now and it is hard to see my paper.

July 17, 1862

Day two on the trail. We went about the same distance today as we did yesterday. The little ones are fine, and the walking is good for Martha. She smiles more than I have seen her smile before. Martha picked some flowers today and gave them to her momma when we stopped. Ashley cried when she held them to her cheek, and I told Martha she had made her momma really happy. She gave Ashley a hug and then ran from the wagon crying. I went after her and held her for a long time while she cried, and I told her it would be alright. But I feel like I am lying when I say that because I know Ashley is dying, but how do you tell the children? Martha is so sweet and little, and when I look at her I feel sad. She will have only a few small memories of her mother too. At least she will have memories. Little Samuel will not.

July 20, 1862

Today we will not travel and so I am sitting alone by the river and dangling my feet in the water. The others are all at their church meeting again, and I did not want to go with them. I went to church once, and it's not something I want to go to again. My momma took me before she left me and when we got home she said we weren't ever going to go again because that old preacher man didn't know what he was saying. And, yes, she might be a sinner in his eyes, but Jesus would understand and he would let her into heaven. She said she did everything for me, and that the love she had for her child was stronger than anything she might do that would make that preacher send her to hell. Well, I was sure surprised by the way she talked and I never wanted to go to no church meetings again and so I was glad when Bart and Alva never went once. I haven't told Ashley this because I'm sure they have a fine church, but it's not for me.

The sun is making my back feel hot, and I wish I could go for a swim, but this is not a good place for that.

I have seen Colier with his mother and I have also seen a younger boy with him that has the same hair and skinny body. Now I'll allow it looks to be a good family because they talk and laugh and they are always smiling. I don't remember ever being happy like that all the time, but I was still little when my momma went away.

July 26, 1862

I am learning a lot here—like you can make fires with stuff that's not wood. They call it buffalo chips and everybody has a big bag in the back of their wagons. Martha helps me gather these buffalo chips from the ground when we see them, so we have fire when we run out of wood. I won't write what they really are.

We got up early today and I made a quick pan of

bread to eat. Today is one of the days when we have cooked with the buffalo chips. They do a good job and put out a lot of heat. I walked for a while this morning when I woke. The children were both still sleeping, and I had to breathe the damp air. I picked the wildflowers that are growing everywhere now. I have never seen such a place as this. It is so wide and long.

I took some of the flowers I found and bundled them together tight and sent them down the stream with a kiss to my momma, just like I used to when I was little. I think that back then, I just wanted her to find them and come back to me. Now I know she will never be back, and I send them so she will know I still love her and think of her. I know she will never get to hold them, but maybe she can look down from heaven and see them and see me.

July 27, 1862

Brother White killed a rattlesnake today. I didn't see it until he took out a knife and just cut its head right off! I remember seeing snakes in the fields when I would go out there sometimes, but never so close. I asked him what it was doing there and why it wasn't so scared of people like most snakes and he said it probably just got all stirred up from the wagons. I told him he was probably right and he said he didn't know about that but it sounded good didn't it? We both laughed then.

July 28, 1862

My fire is dim and I only hope that I can read this later as I am sure my hands are shaking too. It has been a long day and I am glad to let my feet rest. There was a herd of buffalo today like I've never seen before and it about scared me to death before I realized they would not hurt us. The whole earth seemed to be covered with them and they passed right in front of our wagons so that we had to stop and wait for them to get out of the way before we could go any further. We were stopped there for most of the morning and little Samuel didn't like it. He screamed and arched his back so I could barely hold on to him. I walked the ground with him and sang to him and tried everything to get him to settle down until the herd passed and he gave out from exhaustion. Still he sniffled and his body shook now and then as if he was still dreaming about it all. I laid him with Ashley in the wagon and went to look for Martha who became the devil when those buffalo came into sight. She yelled and laughed and ran herself in circles until I couldn't keep up because of that screaming Samuel in my arms. I finally turned her over to a woman who had no children and didn't speak English but she had a kind smile.

After I got Samuel settled, I found Martha in the woman's arms, looking at a picture in a necklace the woman had around her neck. She smiled when I got close but there were no words. Martha still has not said anything to me.

Colier found me as I was walking back to Brother

White's wagon and he talked the whole way. Most of it I didn't understand, but I nodded and pretended that I did so he wouldn't have to say it all again and stay too long. He put Martha on his shoulders and bounced around like a coot—but he got her laughing and by the time we got to the wagon she was tuckered out enough that she fell asleep on the wagon seat by her father. Then he said, "Miss Kate, it sure was good to see you."

He smiled big and said he'd see me again soon. He sure is a crazy thing. He touched the brim of his hat like a gentleman and ran back to drive his family's wagon. I don't know what to think of that boy and I don't have any idea why he insists on staying around me so much—I'm not even a Mormon like the rest of these people here.

I wonder if it could be punishment from that Mormon God because I don't go to his church. But I don't believe that God punishes people like that . . . so I will believe that it was just my own fault for swimming alone and not checking the area before I got in the water.

—From the journals of Cateline Fortier

CHAPTER FIVE
INDIANS

August 1, 1862

I read to Ashley today out of her *Book of Mormon* for only about fifteen minutes and she was crying. I closed the book and said I was sorry I wasn't so good at reading it to her and she said that wasn't it. She told me thank you and said she needed to rest so I left her and went to take care of her children.

Brother White was checking on the oxen when I

left, and when I passed him, he said hello real polite. He asked how I was doing and if I was sorry I came along. I told him, "I'm glad I've been here to help. I think I can do good in Salt Lake City, at least better than I ever would have done anywhere else."

He said, "Thank you for your help," and went to see Ashley.

He walked real slow like he was thinking and I watched him until I couldn't see him no more. He is going to have a very hard time without her.

August 2, 1862

I saw Brother White climb in the wagon with a hand full of wildflowers. The wagon creaked and swayed a little and I heard Ashley telling him thank you and then they were both talking soft and careful and I left to give them some privacy.

August 3, 1862

I am now wrapped in a blanket in the sun and I am still shaking so bad I can hardly write in this notebook today. I have never in my life been as scared as today and I wonder if it could be punishment from that Mormon God because I don't go to his church. But I don't believe that God punishes people like that, no matter what I heard the preachers say, so I will believe that it was just my own fault for swimming alone and not checking the area before I got in the water.

It was so hot and I was dirty from the dust on the trail. All of the Mormons here went to their church meeting, and I decided this would be the best time to go to the river for a bath. I found a place where rocks and logs made a dam and I stripped for my bath. The water sure felt good and I got nice and clean, but then I went down deep in the water and when I came up I saw three Indians watching me!

I was so scared that I screamed loud enough for the whole Church group across the camp to hear me. But then those Indians got big eyes and turned and ran away as fast as they could. I almost drowned in that darn water because my knees were weak and I couldn't get out of the river too fast. I did get out finally and noticed when I was trying to get dressed a big stick stuck in my hair. It poked out on either side of my head and felt like two horns. I had to sit down and laugh even though I was still shaking. Those Indians must have thought I was the devil. I wanted to cry and laugh at the same time, but I was so confused and scared and still shaky.

Brother White came through the trees. I couldn't stand on my own and had trouble telling him what happened. He helped me up from the ground and back to the wagon; he put a blanket across my shoulders and explained to the other men who were running to the river what happened.

They sent out groups of men to watch for Indians, and when nobody saw any, they said I must have scared them good. Brother White sat down and asked if I was alright and talked to me for a minute. He is a real nice man; he made sure I wasn't hurt or too scared before he went off and left to look for Indians, and he even had another lady watch the little ones for a few hours. Now I don't care what those people are all saying because I think those Indians scared *me* more than I ever scared them.

August 4, 1862

Colier came today and said, "Hello Kate." I said for him to sit down and he did. I like for him to call me Kate now.

We even talked for a while and he didn't make fun or tease me or anything until right before he left.

August 5, 1862

Ashley has a fever today, and she feels sick and sore. I wish there was more I could do. I sat for a while with her this morning and she wouldn't eat her food.

Brother White is getting scared of losing her too, I can see it in his eyes and the way he moves.

August 6, 1862

Ashley still will not eat and sleeps almost constantly but not peacefully. She moans and cries at times and the children are scared. They cling to me and will not let me out of their sight. I have tried singing songs and telling stories, and they work for a little bit but then the children get scared and cry again.

August 7, 1862

Still no improvement and I am worried she will die.

August 8, 1862

I sat with the children by the fire until they fell asleep, and then I bundled them in their blankets and laid them down together. They are content, and I worry so much about them and what will happen when Ashley dies.

I have warmed some broth and will take it to Ashley to see if she will sip some of it tonight.

August 9, 1862

Brother White looked all wore out when I went in with the broth last night. He said Ashley's fever was gone and she had talked to him a little bit. I was so glad. Together we got her to sit up and take a few sips of the broth. The effort wore us all out and we laid her back where she fell right to sleep. Brother White told me, "Thank you for all your help."

I said, " I have come to respect your family and

I appreciate all you do for me."

"It's nothing," he replied.

"I never had a family, and even Bart and Alva who raised me didn't ever treat me as good as you and Ashley do."

He got tears in his eyes, and I said I needed to check the little ones.

August 10, 1862

Today is Sunday and I can hear the people singing their songs from here. They sure are pretty, and I wonder how different their church is from the one I went to before. But I don't wonder enough to go and see. I sat for a while and just listened to those people singing. When they stopped I could hear Ashley breathing softly while she slept, and I almost cried to hear how weak her breathing is getting.

Colier came and sat by me while I was writing earlier and I had to put my book away so he would not ask about it. But he saw it and asked about it anyway. I told him it was my notebook so that when I die somebody will know I was a real person and I had dreams. I thought he would laugh, because he is always laughing. But he got as serious as I've ever seen him and looked out across the prairie. I told him I lost my momma when I was four and she didn't leave no record of her life and I wanted to know more about her.

"That's a good thing to do, Kate," he said.

I liked it when he said my name then because he was serious and he was saying something nice.

"My father died on the boat. He was a good man. Maybe I'll go back to my wagon and write about my father so other people will know him too."

I've never seen him like that. Then he looked at me kind of sideways and asked why I didn't go to church. I told him I didn't believe in church and he laughed.

"I don't believe in sitting still for two hours while some old man yells about hell and how everybody is a sinner and damned."

Colier laughed again. He laughed so hard this time that his eyes watered. I pushed him hard and told him to go away, that I didn't want him there and I didn't want to speak to him. He looked kind of hurt but stood up, bowed real low and laughed again. He walked off and I had to sit for a while before I could finish writing about this day.

The people are singing again, and soon they will come home. Only now have I thought about it, but Colier wasn't at church today either!

August 16, 1862

The land has changed so much in the last few days we have been traveling. Now it is all hills, and rocks, and more dust than I've ever seen!

I'm starting to think that there might be something out here after all. We passed a couple of log homes and a telegraph station. It is good to see other people and know they are happy out here. Maybe I will be too.

We stopped early today by the telegraph station. Some of the people from the train went in and sent messages to their families. There was a good well of water there too, and we got Ashley a dipper full and she was grateful. Brother White went with the kids to get them each a drink and I sat with Ashley a while. She asked me to get her book and I did. I started to read and she told me to stop. I asked her if there was something I could do for her, and she said yes. Read that book. I told her she just told me to stop, and she said, "Not to me; read it to yourself. Read the whole thing and when you get done, ask God if it's true."

I told her I couldn't take her book and she said she didn't need it anymore but wanted me to have it. This made my chest swell with hurt because I knew it meant that she would die soon and that she knew it too. She asked me to take care of her children and I said I would take them as long as they needed me. She smiled then and relaxed. She said she loved them and she loved Kirk so much and that he was a good man and a good husband and would need my help. I said I would help and that I would read to her children out of her *Book of Mormon*. She said good and fell asleep.

I will miss my friend.

Ashley did not wake up this morning. She will never wake up again. We will bury her tomorrow.

—From the journals of Cateline Fortier

CHAPTER SIX
LEAVING ASHLEY

August 17, 1862

We stopped early tonight and some of the women around us got their chairs and tables out of their wagons and set up house there on the prairie! There was a big fire built in the center of the wagons again, and people started in with their music before we even finished eating supper. After eating we went to the fire and watched the others dance, Brother White even carried Ashley over for a few minutes and she smiled.

I saw Colier there and he danced with a few girls and I laughed as they stepped on his toes and he tripped over a stick in the ground. He must have saw me because he asked me to dance next and I cleared the grin off my face and said maybe for a minute. We danced for several songs and I know I must have stayed with him for too long. Finally, I said I had to go take care of the children. He left the fire with me and carried sleeping Samuel back to the wagon while Martha walked beside me holding my hand.

That boy sure confuses me the way he can be laughing so hard all the time and then be nice all sudden like.

I think I might like him as my friend if he could be nice like that all the time.

August 18, 1862

We have made good time today and stopped for just a short time about noon for a bite to eat. Some soldiers met us on the trail and said they were headed out to see about some Indian trouble. I stopped one man and asked if they might be close, and he said we would be just fine. I nodded, but I still dream of the three Indians who found me while I was bathing.

August 19, 1862

I saw some dust this morning that had to be from

those soldiers. I wonder where they live and if they like it out here.

August 20, 1862

I sat with Ashley today for a while. Her skin is so white and her hair is thinner than ever. I asked her if I could read to her again from the *Book of Mormon*, and she said please. I asked her if she wanted me to read somewhere specific and she said just open the book and read. I did. The words of Alma to his son Corianton hit my heart hard, and I have to write them down. They made Ashley smile and fold her hands real soft on her chest while she felt the little wedding band around her finger.

This is what it said—*Behold, it has been made known unto me by an angel, that the spirits of all men, as soon as they are departed from this mortal body, yea, the spirits of all men, whether they be good or evil, are taken home to that God who gave them life. And then shall it come to pass, that the spirits of those who are righteous are received into a state of happiness, which is called paradise, a state of rest, a state of peace, where they shall rest from all their troubles and from all care, and sorrow.*

Ashley is going to paradise.

I wonder if she will see my mother.

August 23, 1862

Ashley did not wake up this morning. She will never wake up again. We will bury her tomorrow.

August 24, 1862

Samuel and Martha slept on each side of me last night; Samuel fell asleep easily, but Martha cried for a long time. We did not travel today; instead, we had a funeral for Ashley and a long church service. Martha cried when she saw her mother put in the ground and I cried when she shouted "Momma!" It is the first time I have heard her talk.

Brother White sat on the ground beside the grave when most of the people left and he didn't move. I watched him for a while and worried what I should do. Samuel was asleep on my shoulder and Martha held tight to my hand with more strength than I knew she had. I felt lost and confused and hurt. I finally went back to the wagon and made lunch for the little ones.

How do I tell them they will never see their mother again? I think Martha already knows and Samuel wouldn't understand anyway.

The silence has been terrible today. I cleaned up the children and we went to church. In my mind all I could see was Brother White on his knees by the grave, and I didn't hear a word. Samuel wandered in the grass and picked wildflowers, and Martha sat still next to me on the ground. She fell asleep about halfway through and I carried her to the wagon where I laid her on a quilt to rest. Samuel followed me back to the wagon, and I told him stories until supper time, and then I made a soup with fresh meat that Colier brought by.

August 25, 1862

Brother White came back sometime in the night and he was up before me or the children. He got the oxen all hooked up to the wagon before we even got breakfast ready.

Some men from California passed today. They are headed back east for their families and said they stopped in Salt Lake City. It's a beautiful city with kind people they said—but it doesn't seem to matter now.

August 29, 1862

We stopped at a telegraph station today. It seems so strange how they sit way out here like a reminder that there is civilization. I have a few coins left and thought about contacting Bart and Alva to let them know I was alright but didn't.

What a quiet day. What a slow pace to go and all while leaving Ashley behind.

August 30, 1862

Nights are getting almost cold now. I build up the fire more and sit as long as I can at night before making myself go to sleep. The children are sad and I think Brother White has died inside. I hope there is an end to this mourning.

August 31, 1862

I went swimming this evening to rinse off some dirt. For the first time, Brother White took his children to church alone, so I rushed off to be by myself too for a few minutes. I had barely gotten in the water before I heard someone coming. I hid with just my head above the water near a bush and watched. It was Colier missing his meeting again. I tried to be quiet so he wouldn't see me, but he looked straight at me and then his face got redder than I've ever seen it. He turned around and asked me what was I doing. I told him I was bathing. He said I should come back to the wagons and I told him I had to get dressed first. He didn't talk then for a minute. I asked if he wanted to swim too. This time I heard him suck in some air real loud and he stumbled an excuse about being a boy and a girl and that just wasn't done. I washed my face while he was talking and splashed him with water. He walked away fast and didn't look back.

September 1, 1862

We passed another telegraph station today. Nights are getting colder but the days are still warm. We crossed the Platt River bridge today.

September 2, 1862

Saw a strange sight today called the devil's backbone. We stopped for the night and I went for a walk alone. I came over a little hill and found Colier sitting on the ground watching the sun go down.

"What do you think of this land?" I asked him.

He stood up and turned to face me, but he didn't look at me. He dug a hole in the ground with his foot and turned that bright red again.

"Why is it that you don't go to church either?" I asked him.

He looked up at me funny. I told him he wouldn't have seen me bathing if he was at church. He laughed a little and said I was right.

"Of course I'm right," I told him and walked away.

He caught up to me and took my arm in his hand real soft. He asked if he could walk with me back to my wagon, and I nodded. He didn't say much and I know he was thinking hard about something. We've all been thinking hard lately.

September 3, 1862

Brother White didn't eat supper tonight. I saw him walking alone after he took care of the oxen and he hasn't come back.

September 4, 1862

We passed devil's gate today. The name fits the rocks because by the looks of it, it must lead straight to hell. We passed another telegraph station and camped for the night near the station.

Martha sat in my lap after we ate and said, "Miss Kate, tell me a story."

I squeezed her and said I would tell her all the stories she wanted to hear. She is talking more now and I am glad of it, but when I tried to tell her a story I couldn't think of one—so I pulled out her mother's book and read for a few minutes and Martha was asleep.

I turned the pages to find where it talked about paradise but I couldn't find it so I put the book away and put the children to bed.

It must be the excitement of the bear put us all in a dancing mood and the men in camp all started warming up their harmonicas. Then we were all dancing half crazy through the night.

—From the journals of Cateline Fortier

<blockquote>

CHAPTER SEVEN

THE TALK

</blockquote>

September 5, 1862

The trail has been smooth, and we are on good roads now. There must be a lot of people who travel this way. I wonder if we will be in this Salt Lake City soon. Ashley wanted to go there, but she will never see the place. I feel kind of like a sinner when I think of it because I am hoping they don't make me go to their church. Ashley had lots better reasons for going there and I sure wish she was instead of me.

September 6, 1862

Colier said it won't be long, and everybody is talking about what they will do when they get to Salt Lake City. He asked me what I will do and I told him that I didn't know.

"Where will you stay?" he asked.

"Probably on the street," I answered.

He left then, and I haven't seen him all day. I know I was rude, but I won't feel bad if he never comes to talk to me again.

Just thinking about getting to this city makes me both excited and scared. Will they really take me in, people that don't even know me and have no reason to want me in their houses? Sometimes I wonder if I did the right thing when I went to find my aunt, but this last little while has given me more friendship and love than I've had before. I've seen real families and had friends that I've never had before, and even if I die when we make it to this place, the trip has been worth it.

September 7, 1862

Brother White took the little ones to a short church meeting tonight after we got our wagon set up and the supper cooking. The bread smells good already, and my stomach hurts for hunger.

Brother White came back early tonight and we

fed the children in silence. He barely said a word. After we ate, he kissed them each on the forehead and crawled in his bed. The poor little ones are scared and lonely, and I know Brother White is hurting. I took the children in my lap and we played games with our hands and told stories using fingers, and they laughed until late. I sang them part of a song that I remember from my momma, and they about fell asleep. I put them down and now I am listening to Martha singing that silly song that I couldn't quite remember.

How can I leave these children once we get to Salt Lake City? They are the first I have ever loved completely.

September 8, 1862

We had to take turns crossing the Green River today. We were one of the first there, so I set up our wagon and took the clothes to the river to wash them while we waited. The children played in the trees nearby. I wish we could stay here forever. So beautiful. The children laughed and the water splashed down river until the oxen made it into mud. I even moved further up the river to be away from all the mud. I could see myself living there, caring for Martha and Samuel like my own. They feel like mine and my chest hurts when I think of leaving them. Still I know it will happen, and so I love them now and read to them and sing to them and hold them whenever I can.

I decided to sing as I washed those clothes and Martha came close and sang with me for a while. After we sang just the first part of the song I taught her she stopped and ran after Samuel. Brother White sat himself down by me. I guess that's why she stopped singing. He watched me a while and watched his little ones and then he smiled. I was so surprised I dropped one of his shirts in the river but he caught it before it got away.

"It's good to see them happy," he said.

"It is," I answered.

"I wanted to thank you for all you've done," he said.

I told him that I loved the children and would do anything for them. He threw a rock in the water, and I wondered if I made him upset.

"You did a lot for Ashley too. She loved you."

I wanted to cry for him then.

"I didn't do that much," I told him.

He told me to sit by him and I did. He looked at me for a long time and then at the children. He said thank you again and then just sat there and watched me finish washing his clothes.

I don't know what to think of him. At least he is talking now and I even saw him chase after little Samuel, making him laugh all over. I am glad he is feeling better but I can't help but watch him now; he is amazing.

September 9, 1862

Every day we see something new. Today it is all the hills. So many hills and up and down.

A stagecoach passed us today, and a couple of wagons that did not stop. I had never seen a stagecoach before, so I watched it until it had gone over one of those hills.

September 10, 1862

We stopped at another telegraph station today; the men are all there now. They had to go take an oath of allegiance to the states. It has been a nice day today, and I saw lots of antelope. I might try to kill one later for our supper.

September 11, 1862

I rode out on Brother White's horse yesterday when he got back to watch the kids. I got a good antelope for our supper, and we even shared with some of the other families who wanted fresh meat. Colier found me as I was gutting the animal and he took over, even though he didn't know what he was doing. I sat behind him and smiled, but told him the best way to go. He talked and laughed and I felt real relaxed there with him.

We made it to Fort Bridger today. It's got good buildings and sure was a welcome sight! Brother White got us some potatoes and onions and even a string of dried apples! I made a fine stew with my antelope and some apple dumplings. Those apples won't last long, but they sure do make a body feel better.

I've seen lots of mountains now. They sure are pretty. I've seen snow too—patches of it all over the place—and it makes me cold just thinking of it and more to come.

September 12, 1862

Brother Johnson shot himself a bear today! He even came over to tell me about it! Can you believe it, he came to tell me that he got a bear and I better come see it and get me some meat to try. I did and we just cooked it over the fire on sticks and then ate it right off those sticks. I can't say it was as good as my antelope, but he did a fine job killing it and I said so to him.

It must be the excitement of the bear that put us all in a dancing mood. The men in camp all started warming up their harmonicas, and then we were all dancing half crazy through the night. Brother White held the little ones and said for me to go dance, so I did and there were lots of partners to dance with too. My feet got tired though from all the walking and then the dancing that I was about to sit down but then Colier came along and I started to dance again. He's a fine dancer and a good friend too. I hope I don't loose sight of him when we get to Salt Lake City.

September 14, 1862

Brother White took the children for a walk and invited me to come with them. I packed a lunch and followed them. He carried Samuel and held Martha's little hand. When we got to a pretty little stream we sat down and the children watched for fish and then threw rocks in the water. Brother White laughed and

62

shook his head. It sure was good to hear him laughing and I stared at him hard to see if he was the same man that asked me to come along on this crazy trip.

Then I heard the other Mormons all start to sing, and knew it was time for his church meeting, but he didn't do nothing but watch those sweet children and smile. I smiled too and unpacked our lunch. He ate like it was the best meal he ever had even though it was only some dry bread and salted meat.

September 16, 1862

The children have done really well and I am proud of them. They don't complain and eat most of what I give them. They give me lots of hugs and I think Martha is a angel with her little gifts of flowers or grass or anything she can find.

Samuel said Papa today, and Brother White laughed right out loud! He picked Samuel up and called him his little man and swung him in the air a little. I saw the sadness afterward when he was driving the wagon, and I know he was thinking about Ashley. I sure wish she could see him too because he walks really well now, and he is getting too big for all his clothes. He's just like a little Brother White.

Martha wrapped Samuel in a blanket after they ate and then they both went to sleep early. They must be all tuckered out from walking those hills. It was kind of nice to sit alone and watch the fire, but it was lonely too. I could hear the other families talking, some of them laughing and sometimes there was a child's cry.

It's like being in a big family here, and I've never had a family like it before. Well Brother White joined me by my fire and sat quiet for a long time and we both just watched the flames until they were almost out. He put more wood on and then we talked for a while. We talked about the children and the mountains and the snow. Then we were quiet again and watched the fire until there was nothing left but the coals and then we said good night.

September 21, 1862

Samuel has had a hard time cuttin' a tooth and has been sore and angry lately. Tonight Brother White took him from me while I cooked and rocked the little one for hours while he fussed then smiled and fussed again. When Samuel finally gave out, Brother White crawled under a blanket with him and both of them started to snore. I had to smile at this. I went to my own bed after cleaning out the cook pot.

September 23, 1862

I have never seen much of mountains before, and never anything like these here. There are so many colors in the rocks; it is a powerful thing to see. We have been winding through them all day, and it is a great change from the plains and hills.

Brother White played chase with his children today until they were all so wore out they all lay back on the ground and stared at the clouds in the sky. Martha had so many questions for him that I smiled and left him to answer them all. Like—how did all the rocks grow there so big, and could he give her a piece of that cloud because it looked so pretty and she wanted to keep it.

September 24, 1862

We passed through a place called Echo Canyon. It is so beautiful there and different from anything I've seen! We also passed a few houses and small gardens. The food sure looks good in those gardens. Ours is about gone and we are getting hungry for fresh food.

September 25, 1862

There is a small town near us tonight, and I know we are getting close to Salt Lake City. It makes my heart beat all crazy and I'm scared again. I don't know what to do, so I guess I will go to bed and listen to all the sheep and cattle and hope that I can sleep.

September 26, 1862

We're all tired and hungry now and it will be good to rest.

September 28, 1862

I'm worried. We are so close to this city and soon I will not have the children to keep me busy and happy, and I will have to find my own life. I could not sleep because of the worry, and now I can not sleep because of something else. As I sat by my fire of red coals, all wrapped in a blanket because it sure is getting cold at night, Colier came by. Now I guess I should say that he really is not a boy. He's as close to a man as any. He's older than me and taller by at least a foot. Anyway, he sat down and fiddled with a stick on the ground at his feet and he started talking, asking me what I would do in Salt Lake City. I told him I still didn't know yet. He asked if I would join his church and I told him no. He didn't talk for a minute and then asked me why. I said I didn't believe a person had to go to church to be good and believe in God. He said that was true but asked what if it was the true church? I told him I never heard of such a thing. Well he leaned forward and started telling me all about his feelings for the church and their *Book of Mormon* and I was touched by the way he felt and what he said. He said he cared about me and asked if I could I see fit to look into the church and try it out. I told him I wasn't sure. Well, he talked some more about it and about how his dad died trying to get his family here with the saints because of his beliefs. I told him it would be nice to believe so strong in something like that.

While he talked I could see Brother White sleeping under the wagon with Samuel snuggled up to him.

It made me feel all peaceful and then I heard Colier stop talking.

He kissed me! Just like that he quit talking and just looked at me for a minute and before I knew it he kissed me on my lips! I've never been kissed before and I didn't know what to do or what to say. He didn't either because he said he was sorry and got up real quick and left. Now I can't sleep and I can't get it out of my head. Does that mean he loves me or that he just had to do it? I never even saw Bart and Alva kiss so I don't know what to think and I don't know if I should do anything about it or not.

September 29, 1862

Brother White talked a bit this morning while he ate. He said he heard somebody talking last night with me and asked who it was. I told him it was Colier. He ate some more and then asked what did he want? I said nothing but I knew I was lying and that my face was red and so I said that he just wanted to know what I would do in Salt Lake City. Brother White just nodded slow and I think maybe he wondered too, but he didn't ask.

October 1, 1862

I saw Colier today. He asked how was I feeling and I said I felt real good. He said that was good and he left. I think he is staying away from me because of that kiss.

October 4, 1862

Martha gave me a big hug today and said, "I love you Kate." I told her that I loved her too, and Samuel.

October 5, 1862

We will be there tomorrow, I am sure of it. Now I am more sad than I ever remember. This has been the only time in my life when I had a real family, and now we will separate. I wonder why their Mormon God would do it, first take Ashley and then make me fall in love with these people only to tear us apart too soon. I can't ask Brother White to let me stay with him. Our deal was only that he would get me here, then I would go on my way. Besides, he won't need me anymore. I sure will miss my little darlings though, and so I rocked them late into the night even after they went to sleep. My heart aches, and I am sick.

Colier came by today and we went walking. I told him I was leaving and he got real quiet and pulled me around to look at him. He said he had fallen in love with me and nothing could get me out of his mind. He asked me please would I be his wife.

—From the journals of Cateline Fortier

CHAPTER EIGHT
SALT LAKE CITY

October 6, 1862

We are here! The Mormons all shouted and cried and hugged their families who were waiting, and I wanted to hide. Still I am amazed at this place so far out here. The houses are beautiful, nicer than I've seen anywhere, and the streets are wide and lined with trees! How I would love to live in a house like the ones I see here or just to look inside and see how fine people can live. I have to say I was sure caught up in it all when Brother White called for me. I walked to him slowly, alone because he had his children already. He showed me to a man beside him and told me it was Brother Walker. I said hello to him and he smiled.

"Brother White was just telling me about you and how you helped him," Brother Walker said. I just nodded.

"I know you don't have a place to stay, and I have a room I would like you to have as long as you need it."

I told him that would be just fine and I appreciated it.

Brother White was right about them taking me in. The Walker family gave me a room with a nice bed—a place to live. Now I am in one of those big houses. I asked Brother Walker at supper how he knew Brother White, and he said that he went on a mission and baptized him a few years ago. Now I'm not sure I understand all he means when he talks, and I wonder if he knows I am not a Mormon at all.

October 7, 1862

This house is real pretty. I've never been in anything other than Bart and Alva's little log home, and I feel like I do everything wrong here. The family is nice and I have learned that they take a lot of people in, but none have been like me. They have all been

Mormons and had places to go. I am not and have nothing.

October 8, 1862

Brother White came by today to talk to me. He said thank you again, and I asked him where the children were. He said Martha had a fever and he left her with a friend. He said I should be able to find employment here easy enough and said if I couldn't to come to him and he'd find me a place to stay. I told him thank you, and he shook my hand. He didn't say anything then and I wondered if he might miss me just a little bit. Then he leaned forward and kissed me on the cheek.

I felt that place on my cheek after he left to keep myself from crying.

October 9, 1862

I have heard of some people who are leaving Salt Lake City and are going south. They are going to a small town that I don't know the name of, and I have decided to go with them. I can't stay here forever and this is the fastest way to start my new life.

October 10, 1862

Colier came today and we went walking. I told him I was leaving, and he got real quiet and pulled me around to look at him. He said he was in love with me and nothing could get me out of his mind. He asked me if I would please be his wife. Well I couldn't do it and I told him why—even though my heart pounded and my eyes burned—that I was not a Mormon and never would be. I told him that I knew it wouldn't work because how strong he felt about his church and religion. He said it was true, but if I could just feel the spirit then I would know. I told him to stop talking and that it wouldn't happen, not to me. I told him to find a good Mormon girl to love and he didn't answer me.

He walked away slowly with his head down. He is heartbroken. I am heartbroken.

October 13, 1862

We left this morning to go south. I am traveling with a large group of people who are all friendly but kind of quiet. I have offered to hunt and get meat for the group to pay my way and they said it wasn't needed. They said that I could come and that they had enough to take me where I needed to go. I am surprised by their kindness. I am warm and have the things I brought from Bart and Alva's so long ago. I also have a bedroll that was given me when I went to help Ashley. It isn't much, but I have enough to live. One day, I think that I will even have enough to be comfortable.

October 26, 1862

I have found a family called Pratt who have a store here and a room in the back that is not being used. For helping at the store I will be able to stay in the room. They will also feed me in their house just behind the store. Brother Pratt said he was glad to have me there because they could really use my help. He said there would be extra work sometimes too that might help me put some money aside for later. This was the best thing to hear because I don't want to take from them for long. They are nice, and I don't want to be a burden.

October 28, 1862

These Mormons have more beliefs that I am just now learning—I don't think I like them all. I have eaten at the Pratt's house for a couple of days now and they are all kind and happy people. I thought at first that there were some sisters and their families staying with Brother and Sister Pratt, but today I have learned that all three of the women here say they are married to Brother Pratt. The same man. And they say that it's what God wants them to do. I don't think God would be that way. I mean it just doesn't seem too fair to these women. One of them pulled me outside for a talk and told me all about this polygamy thing. She said it was commanded of the Lord! Now I don't know if I can believe all that, but she does and she says she is happy and she gets along well with the other wives and loves them. She was real nice and all and she gave me a hug and told me that one day I would understand, I just had to ask God for that understanding. I just nodded real slow like and they have not said much more about it. I am glad because it is something I don't want to think about.

I don't know if I should find another place to stay or not. Because I am only going to their house for meals, I might be able to do it. It bothers me considerably and I don't know how they can all live together like that.

October 31, 1862

I have decided to stay with the Pratts. The store is nice and I like to work there. I think I might want one of my own one day. I have been taking on sewing some at night when I am alone and have even set aside a little money. I will use that money to pay for my new horse. She sure is pretty, and Bart would be proud at the deal I made. She was sitting in this little corral on the end of town, and I got to asking about her and found out that the man who owned her had some trouble and up and left the Mormon church. Well some lady had been feeding her and taking care of her, but she didn't want her around no more because she said she had never been broken and she didn't want to fool with her. I told the lady I could handle her, and she was real slow about making a deal because she said I was just a little girl and she could never forgive herself if that horse hurt me. Well that lady finally saw that I was serious and so she said I could take her right then if I would just pay for the feed she had eaten already. I said it was a deal and that I would pay as soon as I could get the money. She seemed pleased to get it out of there but didn't want me walking with it alone. I told her thank you for the worry, nobody ever worried about me much and she smiled and said she didn't know the horse's name and that I'd get to name it myself.

Well, Brother Pratt let me put her in with his horses and I told him I'd work extra to pay for the feed she needed.

I've never had a horse like her, and I know she really isn't much to look at as far as color because she's just a brown horse, but she has three white stockings and she's built right to be a good horse. I will try to settle her down some before I saddle her the first time.

November 2, 1862

My room is warm tonight from the fire I left burning extra long. It is quiet here too and I think that sometimes it is too quiet.

I wonder where the little ones are and if they are safe.

November 3, 1862

I have named my horse Francine. I call her France because that is the place where my mother lived when she was little, and it helps me remember her and not get too lonesome here.

December 4, 1862

I paid for my horse today so now she is really mine! The lady said she mostly ate grass anyway and so she didn't feed it much. I told her thank you again and told her about how I rode her for the first time. She looked glad that I was standing there in one piece and not all broken up.

December 5, 1862

I am still working at the store and it is nice. I like to look at all the store clothes and think if I could get one of those dresses which one it would be. I got my eyes set on some shoes there too and I will get me some one day because the ones I have have hurt my toes for a long time now.

December 7, 1862

It stormed last night real bad, and when I woke up I couldn't get out of my door because of the snow against it. I went through the store instead and got out the front door fine because it has a porch that kept the snow away. It sure was bright outside, and the snow made everything look all clean and pretty.

I got my horse from the Pratts and went for a ride today. I figured that way if she spooked at least I would have a soft landing. But she rode on just fine and she only had trouble sometimes with the reins but I know she will get better over time.

Sometimes I wonder if Brother Pratt has been working with her too.

December 12, 1862

I have found that there are a few single men around here who don't know how to wash or mend their own clothes. I have started to help them and it makes me a little money, but more in the things they want to trade. I am saving the things up for when I have my own house. The money is good too because it will buy the things I need to build my own house with. I hope I can do that this spring.

December 25, 1862

Today the Pratt family invited me over for their Christmas dinner. It sure was a fine meal, and I helped them clean up afterward, and then we sat down and Brother Pratt told the story of baby Jesus. The children all sat close by his feet and listened so well. After the story, they passed a nice gift to each of the children and it was fun to see them smile because of their gifts. Those Pratt women are sure good to those kids. They got scarves and wood toys and some clothes and other nice things.

I told them thank you for the nice meal and started to leave but one of the wives stopped me and said they had a gift for me too. I told them it was alright because I didn't have anything for them and they did enough for me already. Still they gave me a big package and when I opened it I found the most beautiful quilt I ever saw. It was just big enough for my bed and covered with different squares of material to make a pretty pattern. I told them thank you and even cried and gave them all hugs. They asked me to stay the rest of the day with them and I did and it felt real good to be there.

After a while I had one of the children climb in my lap and I told a silly story I remember from my mother. There was no loneliness there tonight.

It is a good way to live and I am happy here but not completely.

—From the Journals of Cateline Fortier

CHAPTER NINE
A NEW HOME

January 4, 1863

It is a new year and the weather has been bad. There is little to do at the store because there are not many customers and so we are making a list of everything we have. It is quiet and I wonder if I will be able to build my house this year as I work. I think I will, but it will be small and I will have to do the work myself. I only have a little money but I'm sure I can earn more before spring, and then I will be able to get a few supplies at least. I think of how it will be to have my own place. I look forward to it, and it makes me work harder.

January 7, 1863

I have not heard from Brother White and expect I never will. I don't know where they are or how to get in touch with them to see if they are well.

February 1, 1863

We had several customers today and it kept us busy for the first time in a while. It must be the sunshine. I wanted to go for a ride on France today, but couldn't because of the work here. Now I am too tired and it is dark anyway.

February 15, 1863

The store was closed today because of it being Sunday and there being church, so I got on my horse while the Pratts were at their meeting and went for a nice ride. The sun was warm, and it felt good to be out and away from everything. I found some pretty places where it would be nice to live, and then I found the perfect spot. It is a little meadow with a creek close by and lots of trees. I'm going to build my house there.

March 5, 1863

I showed Brother Pratt the place where I want my house to be, and he said it was a little too far from town, and I said it wasn't.

"It's not right for a child your age to live so far all alone."

His wives said he was right. I just told them I wasn't a child anymore. Still they said I had to stay with them or move in closer on account of Indians and the bad winters when I would need help. I said that I had been alone my whole life anyway. Which is mostly true because I almost always cared for myself and did whatever I wanted.

He said it was a good place and maybe one day I could live there, but for now I had to be close enough for help to come when I needed it. I suppose he could be right so we followed the creek closer to town until Brother Pratt said I was close enough. I thought it was too close cause I could see other houses from where I stood. He said it wasn't close enough but he would give in if I promised to ride to him when I needed something. I told him my plans for the house and told him I didn't have much money but I had some that I could buy a few supplies with. He nodded but didn't say much.

March 29, 1863

The ground is drying out and I rode out to my land again today. I can just see where my house will be if I look hard enough. I am excited but I'll miss the company of the Pratts once I'm gone.

I stayed all day and walked in the hills and by the river and got lots of rocks for my fireplace. I will go back tomorrow to get more.

April 7, 1863

Brother Pratt said it would be a good day to start on my house and I said I would like that. I asked if he could help me clear the ground some, and he said he could. Well when we got to my land there were all kinds of wagons and people there and I wanted to tell them it was mine, but I saw them smiling and waving to Brother Pratt and I learned that they all had come to help me put up my house. I laughed and wanted to hug them all, but I didn't know them and I said thank you to each of them many times. They just said they were glad to be of some help.

Brother Pratt's wives showed up a little later with some food that sure tasted good after working so hard. I told them thank you, but they made me sit with them a while after eating while the men still worked and they talked about what I would need inside.

I didn't know I had so many friends.

April 10, 1863

I found some material to make curtains in my house. It is not much but it will make it feel like a home.

April 21, 1863

I am alone in my new house! It is done, and it is beautiful. There is a fireplace on one wall that is made out of the rocks I collected, and there is a sawbuck table in the middle of the floor. I put my bedroll on the other side of the room, and I just love the house. I have never had a place of my own, and I feel so lucky to have this.

I built my first fire tonight and the light is soft and pretty on the new walls. It is good to write by, and I know I will be happy here.

April 30, 1863

Today I brought the rest of my things to my house. I now have my mother's things here and the stuff I have been trading for. That is good because I needed a coffeepot, some plates, and a mug. I also got a cook pot too that's made of cast iron like the one I used with the wagon train. I will cook in my fireplace while it is cold, and when it gets hot this summer I will have to make a fire outside to cook on.

But the best thing is that when I was leaving the store with my things on my horse Brother Pratt asked if I had anything to protect myself with.

"What do you mean?" I asked.

He said, "What if the Indians come or some rough men, do you have protection?"

"I will be fine," I replied. "Besides, I can run for help as close as I am to the neighbors."

That was when he got a rifle from the store and said I could pay for it later.

"You've done too much for me already," I told him.

"Don't be too grateful," he answered. "It's old, and I don't know if it shoots straight."

"It will shoot straight enough!" I answered.

"Be careful!" he said, laughing.

May 1, 1863

I made some shelves for the wall where I will keep my flour, sugar, and coffee and all my other food. They look really nice. I made hooks to put on the bottom of the shelves where I hang my big stirring spoon and rags. It doesn't look like much yet, and I know the food won't last me long, but it is a start, and I know I will do good for myself out here.

One day, maybe I can even start my own store in this little house.

May 3, 1863

I shot my new rifle today. If I hold it left and high, it is real straight. It is a good gun and I will do something special for those Pratts one day.

May 5, 1863

I had my first visitor today! It was the wife of one of the men who helped me build my house. She was real nice, and I was glad she came. I told her about wanting to have a store of my own, and she said it was a good thing to do. I said it would take me a while to do because I didn't have anything yet. She said she thought I would do just fine.

I am glad she came, and she said she would be back and she would come when I started my store. I just laughed and told her thank you.

May 8, 1863

I went hunting yesterday and got a small deer. I skinned him and have the hide drying in my yard. I will salt the meat today and hang it to dry. I have decided to keep my hides and take them to the Pratt's store to trade with them for what I need. I know they do lots of trades because I saw it done when I worked there. Brother Pratt is an honest and fair man.

May 10, 1863

I decided that because I have my own house now that I am going to build me a real bed too. I went out today and gathered me some prairie feathers and plan to make a cover to put them all in when I can find enough material.

May 12, 1863

I almost started to think she wouldn't come back, but today my friend came back and she had a few other women with her. I made them some Brigham tea like I learned to do on the wagon train and we all talked for a while. They were nice and friendly and they didn't even ask me if I was Mormon like them.

I like it here.

May 14, 1863

I found some wild greens today. They made a good supper for me with some of my deer that I cooked.

May 16, 1863

I went to the store today. It was nice to see Brother Pratt again. He asked if I liked my new house. I asked him about trading for some dry goods that I might need, and he said he was always there to help and to make a deal.

"Good. I will be back with skins before long and some meat if you'll take it," I told him.

May 20, 1863

I got a basket of apples today for some wash and mending that I did. They were really nice, but I couldn't eat them all just then, so I sliced them and hung them on a string to dry. I will take some of these with me to Brother Pratt's store when I go.

May 23, 1863

I sure ruined some good dresses on that trip here, and I have decided to cut them up and make a nice quilt with them. I will make a couple of bonnets too.

May 28, 1863

I caught some fish for my supper today and they weren't any good. They are full of bones and I almost choked to death on one. These fish are sure pretty to watch swim, but they aren't good like the ones I used to catch at Bart and Alva's.

June 3, 1863

Some man stopped here today and said he knew I traded furs at the store. He wanted to know if I had anything that he could trade for.

"Only a couple of rabbit hides," I told him.

"Let me see them," he said.

I showed them to him and he wanted them. He traded me some fine things and I have put them on my shelf to use when I go to the store.

June 10, 1863

A family stopped here today; they are new and said they were looking for a place to build their own house. I told them that they were welcome and made them some supper. They sure were grateful. After they left I found a little bucket of cornmeal on my front porch.

August 2, 1863

It sure has been a while. I meant to write sooner, but it is busy here so I haven't been able to. I have done more trading, and I even have a few people coming right to my house to see what I've got. Mostly, though, I make things and take them to the store to get by. I have made some soap and candles, and I always take a few hides with me too. It is a good way to live, and I am happy here but not completely.

August 7, 1863

Today the Indians came to trade. I have never been so close to one since they found me bathing on the wagon train. I tried not to look nervous and was glad that one of them spoke a little bit of English. They had a few furs and some pieces of leather to trade and I did my best, sending them out with some cookware, clothes, and some sugar that I was saving for myself. My heart beat hard while they were here, and I had to write about it and hope my hands would stop shaking.

Jesus must sure love the little children! I've never known much of religion or Jesus but this seems right to me and if he loves each child so much, he must love me too.

—From the Journals of Cateline Fortier

CHAPTER TEN
COLIER

August 19, 1863

Many times I have wished for the company of the people I knew on the wagon train, and today I got it. A man rode up to my house and tied his horse out front; I knew who it was when he looked up at the open door. Colier. I couldn't believe it, and I hurried to him and gave him a hug! I pulled back quick though, and we talked for a while. He asked me if we could go for a ride and we did. I should have been more prepared because when we stopped by a stream to visit he asked me about religion and I told him that nothing had changed, and that I didn't want to talk about it. He said he missed me and looked for me everywhere. He said that he still loved me, but he loved his church too and asked me if I could please go and listen and pray about it. I told him I would think about it, and that made him quiet so we had a good day.

August 23, 1863

Guilt got the better of me today and I went to church. I told Colier I would think about it and decided this was the only way to convince him. I have seen where the Mormons meet, so I knew where to go. I went after they started so I wouldn't have to talk to anyone, and I left before they finished so they wouldn't know I was there and think I was serious about this religious thing. I don't want the whole town preaching to me now.

It was different than I thought it would be. There was no yelling about damnation or hell and it seemed calm and kind of peaceful. I think it is the best church I ever heard of, but still, I am a good person and I don't think I need to go just to prove it. I will tell Colier next time he comes that I went to church and we'll see what he says about it.

August 26, 1863

Colier came back and said he was going to build a house in town. I said that it was good, and he said that he would be closer to help me now if I needed it. I said thank you. He said it would be a while before he could come back and see me because of his house and the new job that he got. He didn't even ask me about religion, and I forgot to tell him that I had been to his church.

August 30, 1863

The place seems so quiet and dry. I sat on my porch for a while this evening and if I looked hard enough I thought I could see little Martha and Samuel playing and laughing. How I miss them. How I miss –

September 4, 1863

The weather is bad today. Rain has been pounding down on my roof, and then there's the wind that wants to rock my house and pull it apart. I am glad I brought in wood yesterday so that today I can stay where it's dry. I kept thinking about Ashley this morning and finally I got down her book that she gave me on the wagon train and read some of it. It still confuses me as much as it did when I read it to her, so it didn't last long. Still I like to hold it and think about her and her children. I wonder what paradise is like.

September 9, 1863

The Indians came again. The sun was warm, and I had opened the door to let in the heat and light when they rode up to my house. They came in and looked around, grunted, and pointed. A big Indian went to my bed and looked at everything there real close. He took Ashley's book and started to leave. I yelled at him to stop and he looked at me with meanest eyes I ever saw. He grunted low at me and turned to leave again. Well I didn't want him to have that book so I ran up to him and took it away. He reached out for it and then we just stood there—both of us holding the book and looking at each other. I told him it was mine and he could not have it, and I said it slow and careful. I don't think he understood my words, but he must have known I was serious because he let it go and left my house. The other Indians followed him, and they sure made some noise as they rode away.

My neighbors even came to check on me because of all the noise those Indians made.

September 12, 1863

The leaves are turning colors and I think it will soon be winter. I need to go to town and get some things to get me through it.

September 14, 1863

I rode into town today to pick up some food and dry goods for this winter. My dresses are nearly worn through, and I got some yards of calico and some of butternut color for new dresses. I saw Brother Pratt at the store and he asked me how I was getting along. I told him all about it. He said he would bring his family out for a visit sometime. While I was there, Brother Pratt told me he thought I had a letter. Well that surprised me because I didn't know anyone would want to write me a letter, and then I remembered I even forgot to write to Bart and Alva and tell them where I was. I will do that later.

The letter was from Brother White! My hands sure shook when I opened that letter and read it. I don't know how he found me but I'm sure glad he did. It was so good to get a letter and hear about his children that I have put it here to keep and read when I open this book.

Dear Miss Fortier,

The children have asked about you daily these past months and I have done my best to find you so that I can assure them of your safety.

If the information I received is correct, you are living in your own home and are doing quite well. I knew you would do well here and only hope that you like it as well as the children and I do. I pray this letter reaches you in good health and spirits. Please contact me when you receive this, and I will pass your word to my children who are waiting to hear from you.

We are doing fine. I have secured a good job and have a friend here who watches the children for me while I work. Martha is talking nonstop now and sings like an angel. Samuel is talking as well and he is beginning to put together some good questions and arguments. He is a stubborn little boy!

My thoughts are with you. If there is anything at all that you need, please do not hesitate to ask. After all you've done for me, there is nothing I wouldn't do.

Your Friend,
Kirk White

September 17, 1863

I read that letter so many times, and I still don't understand why it makes me feel so strange inside. He is a good friend, and I have worried about those children so much lately that it must be the relief of knowing that they are well and happy, and that they are still thinking of me. I wrote right back to him and took it to town today. That letter of his sat in the store at least a month before I got it and I wanted him to know I was fine and thinking of them too.

These past few days have been so beautiful. The sun is warm and I have got lots of good vegetables from people who have come to trade.

September 18, 1863

I couldn't stop myself, the thoughts came to me so strong that I pulled out Ashley's *Book of Mormon* and started to read. I didn't even know how long I read until I saw that the light was mostly gone, and that I had read all day. What a wonderful book! For the first time, the words really made sense and hit something in me. I think there has to be something to it.

I read the most amazing story today about Jesus Christ. I know it has to be true because I felt it burn in my chest and I couldn't stop reading for hours. Jesus really came down from heaven and talked to people! He talked about being baptized and he said the people who are baptized will *inherit the kingdom of God*. He said to be like a little child. This I understand because of Martha and Samuel and how sweet they are and how forgiving and kind and loving! Then Jesus blessed everyone! He blessed the poor in spirit, the meek, the people who were hungry or thirsty, the merciful, and a lot more. He talked about joy and rewards. But the most amazing thing that I read today was this: *And he took their little children, one by one, and blessed them, and prayed unto the Father for them. And when he had done this he wept again;—and they saw the heavens open, and they saw angels descending out of heaven as it were in the midst of fire; and they came down and encircled those little ones about, and they were encircled about with fire; and the angels did minister unto them.*

Jesus must sure love the little children! I've never known much of religion or Jesus, but this seems right to me, and if he loves each child so much, he must love me too.

September 20, 1863

Colier came by early this morning as I was just getting up. He said he came to take me to church. I told him that I had already been once and that I didn't want to go again, but he said he wouldn't go without me so he waited on the porch while I got ready and I went with him. After reading about Jesus in their *Book of Mormon,* I have to admit that the church meeting touched me inside. I had some strong feelings but could not admit them to Colier, not yet. I sat stiff and after church he took me home. He stayed for a while, and I made him supper.

September 24, 1863

Colier came by today again. He had a basket and a buckboard hooked up to his horse. He said he would like the honor of my company for the afternoon. I laughed and told him my company wasn't no honor. He said it was to him, and I went with him in his little buckboard. He had a basket full of food and a blanket that he spread on the ground by the creek. We ate and talked about some things we remembered from the wagon train. He told me about England where he is from and explained why he talks the way he does. He told me about his dad and the things they did together, and then he asked me about my parents.

I told him my momma died when I was little, and that I didn't know how and couldn't remember much about her. He asked about my father and I told him that I had never had one.

"Everyone has a father," he said.

"I don't," I replied.

He got quiet then, like he was trying to understand it. I was sorry I had talked so rough to him then and said that it was only my momma and me as far as I remember, and she never did say anything about a father and I had never asked.

Colier tripped then and stepped in the creek, getting his feet all wet, and we laughed hard. He built a fire and took off his boots so they could dry, and we sat on that blanket and talked about other things and laughed and smiled.

I prayed last night for a long time. It is the first time I have prayed that long. I asked about the church and the Book of Mormon and I know there is something to it! I feel so good when I pray and when I read that I know there is truth in it.

—From the journals of Cateline Fortier

CHAPTER ELEVEN
PRAYER

September 27, 1863

I got up early this morning and dressed quickly so that I would be ready when Colier came to take me to church. I have come to like it much better and don't mind going now. He was all dressed up when he got to my house and he had his buckboard and horse waiting outside for me. I do like to see him come; he is a great friend.

September 29, 1863

I made hush puppies tonight just for me. It has been a long time and I ate them like candy.

September 30, 1863

Colier came again today on his way back from town. He brought me my mail, and I was surprised when he gave me two letters. One from Alva, and the other was the one that I was hoping for from Brother White. I put them aside but couldn't keep my mind off them while Colier was there. It is terrible of me, but I think I was glad when Colier left so that I could read them. With both letters in my hands I wondered which one I should open first.

The letter from Alva was short and said she was glad that I was doing well and that they were fine, but the war was bad, and they could hear the guns and feel the men dying. I wish I could comfort her in some way, but I knew I couldn't so I put it down and opened Brother White's. First were two papers with pictures drawn all over them and I cried when I held them. One with Martha printed real big at the bottom and one that said *From Samuel* in his father's writing. It was all scribbles, but I loved it and hung them both on my wall right then. I put Brother White's letter in here again so I wouldn't lose it.

Dear Miss Fortier,

How good it was to hear from you! I read your letter several times to the children and they are begging to see you. Martha sings part of this silly little song every day that she claims you taught her. I really think we need to see each other so you can teach her the rest.

The weather is turning cold as I'm sure it is there, and I pray that you are safe this winter. We have a good home and so I'm sure the children will be safe if not happy. They love it outdoors, and I have to beg them to come inside each evening. They have made many friends and stay busy from morning to night.

My thoughts are with you,
Kirk White

October 2, 1863

The sun still shines warm most of the time, but I know it won't last. The leaves are turning colors and the cold and snow will be coming next. Already the nights are cold and I have put extra quilts on my bed to stay warm. I am worried about being alone this winter. It is my first winter completely alone, and the snow can get so deep. I hope my house can stand the weather.

October 3, 1863

I was cutting wood today when Colier came and took the axe from me. He finished up a good amount and stacked it in the shed. I was glad for the break and sat down and watched him finish. I made him supper after, and we talked about the winter that was coming and if I have enough food to get me through. I don't know what I would do without him.

October 4, 1863

We went on a picnic after church today. It started out so beautiful! The leaves have that red and orange color in them now. We sat down and didn't even start eating before he asked me about being baptized. I told him I can't rush that decision. He said I already had enough time, and that I knew it was true.

"I know there is truth in it, and I will be baptized if I feel it is the right thing to do, but so far, I don't feel like it is," I told him.

He asked me if I had prayed about it yet, and I shook my head. He started to talk real fast then, but I told him to stop.

"I just started reading the *Book of Mormon* and I have only been to church a few times," I said. "I need more time."

He was quiet then, and I told him that I promised to pray about it all, and that I would make the right choice. He smiled then and we finished our picnic.

The ride home was quiet, but he gave me a smile when he dropped me off, and I squeezed his hand.

October 6, 1863

I prayed last night for a long time. It is the first time that I have prayed for that long. I asked about the church and the *Book of Mormon,* and I know there is something to it! I feel so good when I pray, and when I read, I know there is truth in it. I asked God about being baptized, but I don't think I should. Not yet anyway. I don't think I know enough yet about it, and I want to learn more first.

October 8, 1863

Colier came today for supper and I made a fine meal for him. I know he doesn't eat well at his own house and so I try to make up for it when he comes here. We ate good, but I knew he wanted me to tell him that I prayed and that I was going to be baptized. But I couldn't do it, so I stayed quiet and waited for him to ask me. When he did I explained that I loved the book, and the church felt good to me. He smiled, and I hated to hurt him with my next words, but I had to say it, so I did. I told him that I couldn't join his church and I didn't know why it just didn't feel right to me.

We argued. He didn't understand what I tried to tell him, and he said that *he* knew after he went to church and read the *Book of Mormon.*

"Why do you have to be so stubborn?" he asked me.

"I'm not! I really did pray, and that's what I felt! Please don't be angry because it is the right thing for now," I replied.

Well Colier turned away from me and said real low so I could barely hear him, "You know how I feel about you. I love you, and I want you to be my wife, but I will not force you to be baptized, and I will not marry outside of my faith."

My heart hurt to hear these words, and I wanted to tell him that it would be alright, but I couldn't. He said he was tired of being alone and that he was going to take some time to finish his house before the winter got too bad and he would be back later to see me and to check in on me. He left before I could say anything back to him.

October 9, 1863

I returned a letter to Kirk White today. I asked all kinds of questions and felt foolish when I went to mail it. I wrote a short note to each of the children and did my best to draw a picture of my house for them so they could see where I live. I told Brother White that I was reading Ashley's *Book of Mormon* and that I had even prayed some. I told him that I came to the conclusion that there just might be something to it all.

How I hurt today! It took all of my strength to write to Brother White, but I wanted to get a letter out right away. I know that I ruined everything with Colier, and I wish I could feel right about being baptized, but I can't. And I won't do something that important without knowing that I should! I just wish he would give me more time and not push so hard. I do love him, and I will miss him this winter.

October 22, 1863

Colier stopped by today. He brought me some fresh meat and stayed for a quick meal. I told him that I was sorry, and he didn't reply; he just said he had to get back, and he left.

October 25, 1863

It has sure been quiet here lately. I'm tired and didn't go to church today, but I guess that's alright because I don't belong to it anyway.

November 2, 1863

Colier came today again and asked if I needed any chores done. I said I was fine and asked if he would please stay and eat with me. He said he couldn't stay long but he would chop some wood for me if I needed it. I told him I had plenty and he left. I later heard him chopping wood anyway, and I almost went out to talk to him but

I didn't know what to say. So I stayed inside and listened, and when it got real quiet and I knew he was gone I felt bad like I had done something terrible to him.

November 3, 1863

The days are long and cold, and I could not stay home another hour so I saddled up my horse and went to the Pratts' store. I got another letter from Brother White and read it slow, trying to memorize every word. It is so good to hear a friendly word without bothering me about being baptized. That is something between me and God and if he wants me to do it I will but not until he says to and I am ready. I have saved this letter as well, and I know it will be real nice to read on the cold days and nights ahead.

Dear Miss Fortier,

I always welcome hearing from you. You are my greatest strength some days, and I look forward to the day when we will meet again. The children were excited to get your picture and notes. They have posted them on the wall in their bedroom.

Martha continues to ask about you, and asks when she will see you again. Samuel follows and asks to visit as well. I've got my hands full here and I think it would do us all good to visit together.

I am home with the children more during these cold months, and I love to be with them. I must thank you for that, it is something you taught me, how precious these two are. How much joy they can bring to a life! I could not make it without them!

There really isn't much news to write, and I am sure I have taken up enough of your time already so I will close for the time being. You are in our thoughts and in our prayers.

With Love,
Kirk, Martha, and Samuel White

Well I just had to write back so I ran to Brother Pratt's house and borrowed some paper. I wrote a letter right there at their house.

In my letter back, I thanked Kirk White for the letter and said his family was welcome at my home anytime, and I asked him to come and visit as soon as he could. I told him that I sure miss the days when we were on that wagon train and I miss all the people I met because they sure were good people, then I told him how Colier had been around and that he was still a good friend. I closed the letter then because it was getting late. I told the Pratts that I missed them and I would come back to visit longer when I could. Then I hurried to the store and posted that letter. I rode home in the dark and cold.

December 19, 1863

More than a month has gone by since I wrote in this notebook and all there is to say is cold and snow! I am wrapped in the quilt that the Pratts gave me and sitting in front of the fire now with warmth in my body but not in my soul. My neighbors are so busy with their own families that I think they have forgotten that I live here. The weather is too bad to go to town and check for letters, and Colier hasn't been by for weeks. I think I have lost my best friend. But I am sure when the snow stops and it is warmer I will see him again. Maybe then I will even think about being baptized again. Maybe, but only if I know it is right.

I have too much time to think and I wonder could it be true that God would tell men to have more than one wife? I wonder if maybe he did it to somehow protect the women so they would all have a husband and nobody would be left out. These things confuse me, and I wish I could say I knew the answers but I don't. One thing I do know is that if I am ever a Mormon, I will marry a man who is single and he will love only me. Because I don't think I am a good enough woman to be able to share something like a husband.

December 20, 1863

I ran out of wood during the night, so I bundled up to stay warm all night and went out this morning for more.

After being so lonely last night, a miracle has happened. On my porch was a bundle of about five candles tied together with a little bow and a note. *May you have joy in this season of our Lord,* it said. My very first Christmas present! I brought it in and held it for a long time and then untied the bow and looked at every candle. And then even though it was wasteful, I burned one for a while and just sat and watched it.

I don't know how long it was there waiting for me to find it, but the wind blew all night and there were no tracks to see. I sure wish I could thank whoever left them.

December 24, 1863

A great surprise today! Colier came in while I was fixing some dinner and I invited him to stay. He did and said it was very good. I must have talked for hours because some time passed and I don't remember him saying very much. I said I was sorry for talking and that I had just been alone so long that it was good to have him there. I asked him where he was for so long and how his house was holding with all the snow. He laughed a little and said it was just fine, almost as good as my house. He said he didn't dare come sooner because of the storms, but that he was worried about me and had to check on me. I told him I was glad he came and that I missed him and he smiled a little at that. He said he missed me too and wondered if I felt like a picnic. That set us both laughing and the light was almost gone when we stopped. He said he had to go and left real suddenly. The house is sure empty without him here.

January 10, 1864

It is a new year and it is cold. Next year I will not be so cold. It is not just the outside of me but I am so alone and that is what makes my bones and my heart feel it too.

February 5, 1864

I finished my calico dress today, and it fits real nice. I will wear it this spring when I go to town.

February 20, 1864

I have a new skirt made from that butternut material. I will make me a shirt to go with it when I cut up these old dresses.

March 2, 1864

It is spring! The snow is nearly melted and the sun is warm on my back. I have had enough of staying in my house, so today I went out on my porch to watch the world turn green again. There was not much to write over the long winter months and I am glad it is over. I spent most of the cold months reading and sewing. I even read the books of my momma's. I have a new dress for myself too.

I think I will go to town tomorrow. I am ready to get away and could use more supplies for this spring.

March 4, 1864

I got another letter from Kirk White! It sure made my heart sing to get that letter, and I am even more excited because he said he is coming to visit—next month if I don't mind. I am happy today. I wrote back to my friend and told him to come whenever he could and stay as long as he wanted.

Oh, what a beautiful day it is! I rode home with the sun on my back, and then I even rode up into the hills just to get out and be away for a while. I love the smell of spring and the animals that come out from everywhere.

March 6, 1864

Colier came for a visit today. He asked me all about the winter and how I made it and if I was alright. I answered all his questions and asked him about his winter and house. He told me all about it. We talked for a while but there was a distance there that I haven't felt with him before, and I hope that doesn't mean he will forget about me. He asked if I read more from the *Book of Mormon* and I said that, yes, I did. He asked what I thought about it, and I explained it to him and said it was a great book and told all about Jesus and wars and good men and bad men and I think it has some great lessons to learn. He nodded and asked if I prayed about being baptized again, and I said that I did. He leaned forward with his elbows on his knees real interested.

"Well?" he asked.

"I won't be baptized yet, but it all looks really good. If God wants me to be baptized then he will let me know and I will do it," I said.

He didn't like my answer, and he wanted to say more, but he shut his mouth real tight and left for church. He didn't ask if I wanted to go but that is alright because I didn't feel comfortable with him just then.

I want to cook for more than myself and I want to hear Kirk chopping wood and whistling as he feeds the horses. I want to hear the children laughing and singing and I want to see every smile.

—From the journals of Cateline Fortier

CHAPTER TWELVE
VISITORS

March 20, 1864

I talked to Colier today at church. He talked real nice and I told him about the Whites coming to visit and said he should come over and see them while they were staying at my house. He didn't look excited like I thought he would be and just asked if there was a reason for their visit. I got a little angry then and said they were friends and didn't need a reason to visit. He said something then that I didn't hear and I hurried home to get my house ready for company.

April 1, 1864

I have been so busy lately with my house and the sewing and wash. I want everything to be perfect when my visitors arrive, so I have emptied my house and cleaned it completely. I have organized my shelves and tried to stock them as best I can. I don't want to run out of food or have them think I can't feed them while they're here. I want room for the little ones to play and places for them to sleep. I even borrowed some quilts from the Pratts so that my floor won't feel so hard to them.

April 2, 1864

Colier came to my house today and fixed my roof for me. I was terribly grateful and made supper for him. He said that he was sorry for the way he acted at church before, and that he would like to come see the Whites when they came. He said the children must have grown and he wondered if we'd know them at all and we laughed about it. I showed him the pictures the children drew for me and he thought they were fine. He said he would like to take me to see his house soon, and I told him that I'd like that.

After Colier left, I sat in front of the fire and thought and read. I sure do like that *Book of Mormon* now and I understand a lot it says.

April 10, 1864

Colier came over today with a bundle of wildflowers and took me to church. After church he took me on my first picnic of the spring. We had a grand time and even did a little fishing. I told him that I sure did like to fish, but if we caught anything he would have to eat it. He laughed.

When we got back to my house he said, "I almost forgot," and gave me my mail from town. He said that he picked it up a couple of days ago because he knew I wouldn't be in for a while longer and that I'd want it. I thanked him and even gave him a hug. He left then and tipped his hat real nice. Well I had two letters again and I read them quick and read them again.

Dear Miss Cateline Fortier,

It is with great anticipation that I write at this time. I have secured my home and taken leave of my work so we may come for a time to visit. The children never tire asking of you and I pray we travel safely as we come to your home.

I do hope we will not cause undo burden. We continue to pray for your safety and happiness.

With love,
Kirk, Martha, and Samuel White

I will have my friends here soon! I have included my letter from Alva as well.

Dear Cateline,

It is with deep regret that I write to you today. My dear husband, Bart has left this world.

You know that we are only poor farmers that live on southern soil; we have no fight with anybody and have tried to live to help all. I suppose that just living in the South was enough to make us enemies. I have never been so scared as when those Yankees came to our home and took what they wanted. Poor Bart had no chance of defending our home or our food and was buried the next day by my own hands.

Our home is intact and has given me shelter through the harsh winter and for this I am grateful. You are most fortunate that you left when you did. You saved yourself.

Alva

I read it over a few times and then decided to write back and ask her to come live with me. I had room and she would be made welcome as I had; I knew it. If she could just get as far as Salt Lake City, I could pick her up there, maybe borrow Colier's buckboard to carry her home in. Oh dear Alva who never showed me the motherly love like I wanted but did have respect for me and taught me so much. I have to do what I can.

April 11, 1864

What a happy day! The best that I ever remember! I was in my kitchen making a small pot of stew when I heard a voice behind me yell Kate! The next thing I knew I was grabbed around my waist by a much bigger Martha than I remember. Oh how I loved her, I picked her up and held her for so long—afraid that if I put her down she just might leave me again. How could I ever let her leave me again? How can I live without her after such a beautiful day with her once more? I saw such a big boy standing just inside the house by the door and after setting Martha down, I took my little Samuel and cried. Such happy tears for the ones I missed for so long. They both talked at once and told me all about their trip, and Martha said her father was taking care of the horses and would be in soon.

Nothing could have prepared me for the sight of Kirk White after such a time. I wanted to hold him like I held the children; I wanted to touch his face to be sure he was real and to assure myself he was the same man. I wanted to cry for happiness and make him promise not to leave ever.

If anything, he was more handsome. I had to swallow suddenly and looked at the fire where my stew must have been burning.

"I only made a little," I said, "but I will make some fresh corn bread to go with it, and it should be enough for us all."

I must have made a fool of myself, falling all over the children and then not even able to look in his eyes as he stared at me because he didn't say a word. He didn't talk for the longest time, and then he cleared his throat and just said, "It is sure good to be here."

After supper I showed him around and he talked about everything. He said I had done well for myself and that he was impressed.

"Thank you," I told him, "but I had a lot of help."

I took him in my very small house again and said that I didn't have a lot of room, but we could make beds for him and the children on the floor by the stove so that they could stay warm at night. He said that would be real fine and just looked at me again, and I worry now that the floor is not good enough for him and his children. I wish I had a better place for him, a good bed at the very least.

April 12, 1864

I didn't know happiness could last so long. All night I could barely sleep because of it and it was just as strong this morning! I wanted to get up early and wake those beautiful children, to tell them stories and take them for a walk to the creek and show them my horse and—

I asked Brother White what he wanted for breakfast this morning and he came real close and looked down at me for a minute. Then he said real low that he thought we were good friends and asked if I would I please call him Kirk. I told him alright and had to take a step back because suddenly I felt that I couldn't breathe with him so close—I don't know what is wrong with me. I got down the flour and turned my back to him and said that he better call me Kate then.

I told the children stories during the afternoon and hugged them close. Then I put them down for a nap. I hope I am not trying too hard, but it feels so good to have them here.

April 13, 1864

We had a picnic by the creek today, and I took both children for a ride on my horse after dinner. We went into the hills, and I showed them my favorite spots to go and some good places to hunt. Samuel fell asleep on the ride, but Martha asked questions about all of it and she sure made me smile for the rest of the day.

We must have worn those children out today because they fell asleep early and I went out to the front porch to sit a while. Kirk sat next to me after a minute. We didn't talk but stared at the stars and the trees around us. Then Kirk broke the quiet and asked me about my family, where they were and what had happened to them. I told him everything that I could remember. I told him that there never was a father and my momma never once said anything about him so I didn't know who he was or if he was alive. I felt real comfortable with it, not like anyone else I ever told. He nodded a lot during my story and just said that it must have been hard on my momma not having a man around to help and he said she must have been a good strong woman. I said that she was and told him how I remembered her singing all the time and remembered her laughing and telling stories and jokes. Then I told him how she never came home, and I was sent to Bart and Alva.

He took my hand then like it would give some of his strength and it did. I asked him questions about his family and how he met Ashley and how he decided to come to this place. He answered all my questions, and then he thanked me.

"I have never seen my children so happy. You're good for them. I wish we lived closer," he said.

I wish for that too, but I didn't tell him. A breeze came along and we got cold so we went in and said good night.

April 14, 1864

Another wonderful day with the children. I woke up to smell flapjacks cooking, and Kirk just smiled when he saw me up. He said that I looked tired and he thought he'd help, and I said thank you. The children slept so I sat and watched him cook and then ate while he finished up for the little ones.

April 15, 1864

Colier came by today just after breakfast. I was washing up the dishes and Kirk was chopping me some wood. The children were in the kitchen singing with me and we were trying to remember all of the words to my momma's songs. I saw Colier out the front door and went out to say hello to him. He was talking to Kirk real low so I couldn't hear and when Kirk saw me he smiled and walked over. Colier looked at him and then at me and I saw something like fire in his eyes for a second. He said it sure was good to see Brother White again and asked when would he be leaving. Kirk said it was up to me and I smiled and said he could stay forever if he would let me love the children every day. Colier said good-bye, and then and rode away.

I told Kirk that I was sorry and that Colier usually was a lot nicer than that and usually stayed much longer. He nodded then and kind of smiled so I asked what it was all about. He said Colier was jealous, and I asked of what? He said that Colier liked me and didn't like to see me talking with another man. I kind of shook my head, and then I decided I probably should tell him about Colier asking me to marry him. When I did, he asked me what I had said. I told him about our trouble with religion, and he kind of laughed and looked away at the mountains.

April 16, 1864

I am so tired. It must be that I haven't had more than a few hours of sleep in the last several days, but I don't want to miss a thing. I don't want to be sleeping while the children are awake and I don't want to sleep so I can watch them sleep. I want to sit on the porch and watch the night with Kirk and talk to him. I want to cook for more than myself and I want to hear Kirk chopping wood and whistling as he feeds the horses. I want to hear the children laughing and singing and I want to see every smile.

I was so caught up in the words of the book that I didn't notice that Kirk was there until he gave me a cup of coffee. I smiled at him and said thank you. He sat beside me and his arm brushed against mine and made me shake inside. Could it be that I am falling in love with him?

—From the journals of Cateline Fortier

CHAPTER THIRTEEN
BAPTISM

April 17, 1864

I felt something very real in my chest at our church meeting today. Samuel slept on my lap, and Martha sat between me and Kirk. The man speaking talked of Jesus and about the pain he suffered so that we could one day live with him again and be free of our own sins. Wow. I look back at my life and my own sins; they may not be big ones but they are enough that I worried sometimes that God wouldn't want me around, that I wouldn't make it into heaven or the paradise where Ashley is. He said that Jesus loves us, and I know he does because I read all about him in the *Book of Mormon*. He loves all people and heals them—especially the children. I think this is a good church, but still I will never be able to share my husband like the Pratts if one day God sees fit to give me one.

Martha walked real slow after church and I stopped to ask her if something was wrong. She looked up at me crying and shook her head real big. She said simply that her Momma was in heaven but she still loves them and one day they will all be back together forever. Then she smiled at me and said that her mother loves me too because Martha heard her say so. And she told her Daddy that and said that she wanted me to stay with the children always and that he should help take care of me if I needed it. I asked her if she was sure her momma said all that, and she nodded and gave me a hug. Then she asked if I would stay with her forever too. Well I didn't know what to say to her because I sure love her, but me and her dad have different lives, so I said that I love her too, and if there was any way I could then I would do it. She kissed my cheek then and started skipping ahead of me.

April 18, 1864

I couldn't sleep last night and so I lit a little candle and read almost all night. I felt so good and understood most everything I read, and it really made a lot of sense. I only have one big problem with this church now but if God tells me that it's true and I need to be baptized, I think I am ready.

April 19, 1864

Another wonderful day, but with some sadness to it because I know I will only have my visitors for another day or two. I tucked the children into their beds tonight and watched them until they were breathing real quiet and peaceful and then I just couldn't stand it. I started to cry and couldn't stop. Kirk came and sat beside me and asked me what was wrong. Well I couldn't stop to say, so he pulled me close and just held me and I rested my head on his shoulder and felt his warmth and strength and his comfort. I prayed in my heart then that he would stay with me forever, but I knew it wouldn't happen. I prayed that I would know what to do and then it came to me so clear that I sat straight up and looked at him serious. He was confused then and apologized for being so forward. I said it wasn't that and told him that it was like a voice just came into my head and told me that it was true.

He asked, "What is true?"

"Your church," I said.

He smiled a little and reached for my hand. I let him hold it and leaned toward him and whispered real fast that I knew I had to be baptized.

"I don't know why I had to wait this long, but God didn't tell me to do it until now, and he said his church is true. I believe him, so I will be baptized."

Kirk reached up and touched my cheek and then pushed the hair from my face. I told him to please stay a couple more days, and he said if it was so important to me that he would. I said it was.

"I want you to baptize me before you go home," I told him.

April 20, 1864

Kirk told the children about me getting baptized and they were happy and gave me hugs. He told them that he was going to do it and that they would be staying a few more days. They danced around then and we all started dancing around the house, and then we knelt and prayed together and I could feel a strong burn in my chest. I cried through the prayer that Martha said.

April 21, 1864

I woke up feeling peaceful and calm all over. The children were asleep and Kirk was sleeping so I got my *Book of Mormon* and went to the porch where I read for maybe a hour. I was so caught up in the words of the book that I didn't notice that Kirk was there until he gave me a cup of coffee. I smiled at him and said thank you. He sat beside me and his arm brushed against mine and made me shake inside. Could it be that I am falling in love with him?

Well, we had lunch but I couldn't eat anything

because I was too excited. We went to the creek then where it was all dammed up and the most beautiful thing happened. I bet the whole church came and they stood on the bank and watched with smiles as Kirk said the words that cleaned me and made me a Mormon. He shook my hand real formal after and all the Pratt women gave me a hug and some other ones too. It didn't matter to them that I was all wet. Martha started to sing a church song and then everybody joined her and I never wanted it to end, the songs and the feelings and the friends.

A man named John asked to dance with me and he was good too. I felt real pretty as he twirled me around and smiled at me. He asked me my name and some other questions and seemed right pleased when I told him I just was baptized.

—From the journals of Cateline Fortier

CHAPTER FOURTEEN
THE DANCE

April 21, 1864

Kirk left this morning with the children. I cried. I've never felt more alone than when I came back in the house and found it empty. No Martha, no Samuel, and no Kirk. I know they are not in the yard playing to return any minute, but I wish they were. I wish I could look out the door and see Kirk chopping wood or chasing the little ones around. I miss them so much already.

There is a new feeling here now, it comes from deep inside and it is peace. I feel love there and understanding, and I can pray now so easy and know that I have done the right thing. I am understanding much more of the church now and the ways of the Mormons and it is a good life. The teachings are good and I am glad that I am in this church.

April 22, 1864

I walked to the creek today and took a nap on the bank. I watched the fish swim for a while and then scared them off when I threw a rock in.

April 24, 1864

I went to church alone today and so many people smiled at me and said hello and asked me how was I doing. I answered them and said a quiet prayer of thanks to God for all of my friends and the feelings I have.

Colier came then and sat by me. He took my hand and looked at me for a minute before he said he was proud of me and congratulations. I told him thank you. He asked if I would mind if he sat next to me, and I said it would be just fine, so he did and I listened so very careful to everything they said and I felt it burn in my heart again and I am glad. When church was over Colier asked if he can come by and see me sometime and I told him I would like that. He smiled then and said good-bye. I walked home alone to an empty house and felt the sad come back again. It is hard to be here and not hear other voices now.

April 27, 1864

Some women from my new church came by today and visited with me. It was nice to have somebody to talk to. They didn't stay long though because of all the chores they have at home and their children. I told them to come back anytime and they smiled and said they would.

April 28, 1864

I made a fine stew today and bread. There is so much and nobody to share it with. I don't know what I was thinking.

May 3, 1864

Colier came by today like he said he would. It was good to have his company, but it is not the same friendliness there that we had once. He chopped wood before he left and I watched him but it was not the same as watching Kirk and I felt empty and tired. I went in the house then and listened and wished that when it ended Kirk would come in and I would give him a smile and feed him. When the chopping did end, Colier came in and we shared some fresh bread and he left with a kind smile and a tip of his hat.

He is a fine-looking man and will make somebody a good husband one day.

May 20, 1864

A month has passed and there has been no word from Kirk or the children. I pray that I did not do anything to offend him while he was here. I think about it and wonder if maybe my last letter did not make it to him. I will write another and post it today.

May 22, 1864

Colier came by and offered me a ride to church. I said that I would like that, and he waited while I got ready and climbed in his buckboard. We sat together during church but I couldn't listen because my mind was with Kirk and the children, and I wanted to talk to him and to know that he was alright. I wanted to see him again and to tell him that I was sorry if I had done anything that was not right. I was surprised when the meeting ended and I didn't hear one word. Colier took me home but before he did, he stopped by some trees where it was real pretty. He said he was real proud that I was baptized but he looked a little sad when he said it and I wondered if he wanted to be the one to baptize me instead of Kirk. I felt right about my decision, but I listened hard to his words. He said he was ready to marry and now that I was a Mormon he would like me to reconsider his offer of marriage.

I should have expected it, but it really took me by surprise and I didn't know what to say to him because my feelings told me that it wasn't right. A voice told my mind that there was somebody else for me and somebody else for him. I looked at him sad and he told me not to even say it. I told him that I loved him and that I would never have made it without him but that I couldn't marry him because it wouldn't be fair to him.

"What do you mean?" he asked.

"There is another girl somewhere waiting for you," I replied, "and she will make you so happy, and I can't take that away from you."

Well he slapped the reins across the backs of the horses, and we started again. I told him that I knew there was someone he would be happier with, but that I would never forget him. He didn't answer me, and I said that I would always love him and never forget him. He came to my house and stopped. After he helped me down, he left real fast, and I felt like I had just hurt him as bad as I ever could. I wish he hadn't asked me again. I think it would have been better that way.

May 26, 1864

I got a letter from Alva today.

Dear Cateline,

Thank you for asking me to come, but I will never leave my home. I am an old woman now and no move will change that. I have nothing and nobody to share it with. I look forward to the day that I die and depart from this dark world.

I wish you the greatest happiness. Marry, have children, and love them. Please do a better job than I ever did with you. Thank you again.

Alva

June 1, 1864

I couldn't stand the house a minute longer so I went to town today to get away and in my hopes, I asked about any letters for me. I was prepared for disappointment but was happy when Brother Pratt handed me one delivered that morning from Kirk. I told him thank you and he laughed and said it wasn't him that done it but he hoped it was good news that I got. I said I was sure it was and I left his store to sit by the street and tear it open.

I am somewhat disappointed by what he said, or I guess I mean by what he didn't say. It was good to get the letter, but it just wasn't what I hoped it would be. I don't even know what it is I wanted to hear! I rode home from town then and smoothed his letter in these pages.

Dear Miss Fortier,

I wanted to write and assure you that yes, we are all well. We have been busy getting caught up from our visit to your home and have been unable to write before now.

I also wanted to thank you for your hospitality.

Sincerely,
Kirk White

June 4, 1864

I wrote back to Kirk, or should it be Brother White as he is being so formal with me? I told him that I am well and that he is still welcome at my home whenever he wants to come. I told him to bring the children again because I miss them considerably, and I hoped I didn't offend him by anything I did while he was here. Then I told him about church and about the weather and about Colier coming by and asking me to marry him again. I said also to kiss the little ones for me and tell them that I love them and want them to be happy forever.

June 5, 1864

I stayed the night with the Pratts and had supper with them and all their children. It was nice to hear all the voices and the laughter, and I am glad I stayed, but I'm sad too.

I went to church and ate with them and then rode home alone. It really isn't too far between our houses, and I think I will go to visit them again soon.

June 7, 1864

Some Indians came again today. I have got more used to them now, but I still get nervous when they are here. We did a little trading, and I did real good. I smiled and said thank you when they left. One man gave me a little wave as he rode away.

June 12, 1864

I went to the creek today after church. Some folks asked me to come for dinner, but I told them I had a few things that couldn't be put off and I would have to do it another day. They said that would be fine and asked me to plan on next Sunday. I said that I would like that. I took Ashley's book with me to the creek and I sat there and read for a long time. I felt good inside and then I prayed for a while asking God what

I was supposed to do with my life. I didn't hear any great shouts of instruction, but I felt good and even a little happy.

I think he has something planned for me, but I wish I knew what it was so that I wouldn't worry so much.

June 13, 1864

I wrote back to Alva today, and I know I will never hear from her again. I just had to tell her thank you for all she did for me because she did teach me a lot of things and she was good to me. I told her that I was sure sorry that she wouldn't come but that I understood how she didn't want to leave her home and the pretty country out there. I told her that somebody did ask me to marry them and one day I would have children and I would tell them about her and my life growing up there. And then at the end I even said that I loved her.

June 30, 1864

Another letter from Kirk.

Dear Miss Fortier,

The children were excited to know you are well and asked to send you these pictures. Please accept my congratulations on your engagement. I know you will be happy with Colier. He loves you, I could see it in his eyes when I was there.

Sincerely,
Kirk White

I had to put that letter in here to explain, I forgot to tell him that I told Colier no. He thinks I am getting married and now I feel like I have made the biggest mistake ever! I wrote right back to him and explained that I meant to tell him what I told Colier and I wrote a letter for each of the little ones with pictures of the sun and stars and silly things.

July 1, 1864

I read Kirk's letter again today and it made my stomach feel sick. I can't believe that he thinks I am getting married.

July 5, 1864

I went to a dance last night. I had to do some thinking before I went and I almost stayed home anyway. I wore the new calico dress I made while it was winter, and it looked real nice. Some folks from our church have got themselves a real band with fiddles and guitars and a banjo and they all sing so pretty and fun. It put us all in a dancing mood right away and I don't think anybody sat out more than a dance or two—even me. Colier was there and he said it was good to see me and introduced me to a girl named Susan. She sure was pretty. She said hello and asked me a few questions. I liked her right away and told her that I hoped we could visit more later. She said she'd like that and they danced together for most of the time and then I didn't see them anymore; they must have gone for a walk.

A man named John asked to dance with me and he was good too. I felt real pretty as he twirled me around and smiled at me. He asked me my name and some other questions and seemed right pleased when I told him I was just baptized. He asked where I lived and if he could call on me sometime. I said I would like that. Then I danced with Ammon and he said he was born in Salt Lake City.

I said, "That must be something."

He said, "It sure was. My family was one of the first to come, and my mother almost didn't make it across the plains."

"I'm glad she made it," I told him, and he smiled at me and we danced some more.

There were others, but I don't remember their names, and then I danced with John again.

It was late and too dark to go home when the dance was over so I stayed the night at the Pratts' house. They sure do their best to make me feel at home there, and I have to admit that they all do look happy. Maybe it's not such a bad thing to share a husband if you find a real good one.

John came over right after we had breakfast this morning and asked if he could ride home with me. Brother Pratt said he thought that would be a good idea—so John saddled up my horse and we rode together and talked and I laughed at his stories. It sure was a fun day, and I asked him if he could stay for dinner. He said that he had some things to do in town but would be back tomorrow to take me up on that meal.

July 6, 1864

John came and we had dinner just like he said he would. He was real polite and talked nice and soft and he thanked me for the meal like it was the best he ever had. I think he just doesn't get too many real meals like that. After we ate, we went walking around my place and he asked all kinds of questions. We had a nice time and I was sad to see him leave.

July 8, 1864

Colier came today and said he wanted to thank me for my friendship and that he was getting married. I asked him if it was to Susan and he nodded big like a little boy would. It reminded me of the first time I met him, when he was laughing so hard. I told him I was happy for him and that he should come to me if they ever needed anything. He stopped at the door when he was leaving and looked at me for a while, and then he kissed me on the cheek real quick and said thank you again.

I know he will be happy.

July 10, 1864

I had dinner with some folks from my church today. They talked about Colier and Susan and they thought it was such a great thing too. John was there and it was real nice to have his company to keep my mind busy again. We went walking for a while after we ate, and I am worried he will want to ask me to marry him too. He is a good friend, but I don't know if I will ever love him.

Sister Pratt said that John is sweet on me and I hope it's not true.

He asked if I would love his children forever, if I could take them and raise them as if they were mine. I nodded. He asked if I could care for them and love them always even after I had children of my own and I nodded again.

—From the journals of Cateline Fortier

CHAPTER FIFTEEN
THE PROPOSAL

July 13, 1864

Finally another letter from Kirk. Even if he has resorted to a more formal matter in his letters to me, I can't see him as anything other than Kirk, and he will always be. I got two beautiful pictures from the children that I have hung on my wall and a letter from Kirk, the letter I have included here.

Dear Miss Fortier,

I was pleased to get your last letter and wish to assure you that you did nothing at all to offend while we were at your home. On the contrary, you seemed to do everything right. I have not seen the children as happy.

I wish I could provide some amount of caring and love to them that you seem capable of, but I believe that is the place of a mother and a man can never be all they need.

I pray for your safety, and the children do as well. They love you and they will never forget you. I will never forget you. Please accept my sincerest apologies for making you somehow believe that I may be angry or offended. I stand in complete amazement at all you have been able to accomplish and maybe it is simply my admiration that made me feel inadequate and unable to reply directly after our visit.

My thoughts are with you.
Kirk White

What a letter! I feel so much better knowing there is no need to worry about what I may have done, and the letters and pictures sure did a wonderful thing to my spirits! I nearly flew home after posting a letter of my own. I told him about the dance and about Colier getting married so sudden, and I asked him to come again and told him to take good care of the little ones. I told him that he was a good father, and he gave those children all they could ever need and more, and they were lucky to have him.

It was hard to stop writing but I did and handed the letter over to be mailed and then I think I ran France all the way home and then past my home and into the hills, where we stopped and played in a stream until it was late and the air was cool.

July 14, 1864

John came today, and I sure didn't look my best! He came while I was chopping wood and I was sweaty and dirty and my hair hung like moss in my face. He smiled and said to go get cleaned up he had plans for me, and he took the axe away. He thumped it in a log and sat on the front porch while I went inside and washed and changed. I didn't feel all nervous like I did sometimes with Kirk. I wondered if maybe that was a good thing. Maybe that meant that we were supposed to be together because then I could really be myself and not worry about my mind getting all addled. He really is handsome, and he sure is strong enough to be a good help around a place. I thought about it for just a second and then I shook my head. He was my friend and I sure did need one.

We went for a walk down a trail and he stopped where there was a blanket all spread on the ground.

He said he was sorry that he wasn't a better cook, but he wanted to be sure and repay me for the meal that I had made for him. I said he didn't need to, but he said he wanted to do it. I sat down and we talked about a lot of different things. He didn't laugh like Colier always did, but he was kind and he had a nice smile that made me feel good.

July 17, 1864

I missed church today but read for hours in my book. I know that doesn't quite make up for church, but I couldn't sit through it today.

It sure has been quiet and I have prayed a lot and wondered what I will do in my life. I wonder if I will ever have a family. I feel that I will, but don't know how soon. I guess I am still young, but I won't be forever.

I have been doing wash and mending for John. He pays me good and always stays to visit when he drops off or picks up his clothes. I tell him I hate to take his money but I don't have much choice, and he laughs. He usually stays to eat with me too and this makes my house not quite so lonely.

July 21, 1864

I finished another blouse to wear with my skirt. It looks real nice, but I have nowhere nice to wear it.

July 27, 1864

It sure has been a quiet time, and I have spent most of it hauling water from the creek to my little garden. It is a sad garden and I will be surprised if anything grows in it. The sun has been hot and the leaves all look a little yellow and dry. I have never had to worry about all this dry before when I was helping Bart on his farm, and I wasn't sure what to do about it. Then John showed up the other day and said he would rig up a watering system from the well to my garden for me and it would sure make it an easy thing to water it. He has been good to me and I think I could make a nice life with him.

I have been tired today, and I think that tomorrow I will leave for a while. The horse needs some exercise and I could use fresh meat so I will go for a ride tomorrow and bring back some deer maybe.

I wonder if John will want more than one wife. It is something we need to talk about if he asks me to marry him.

July 28, 1864

I went for a ride today, and it was so good to be away from the house that I forgot all about hunting and just rode for hours. I found a nice pond that had warm water and I took a long bath there too. I laid out on the grass after and dried off—then I picked up this notebook and decided to write. Yes, I do take it just about everywhere I go, but it is my story, my life, and I don't want to leave anything out.

It sure is pretty here. There are wildflowers everywhere, and the trees are green and tall. But the snow comes sooner and it stays so much longer. It would never be a good place to live so I just visit when it is warm and stay as long as I can. I wonder if this is how it looks at Kirk's house, or if his is in one of those places where everything is dry and dead. I have never even thought to ask him about all that. I think I will write to the children and ask them to draw me a picture of their house.

July 29, 1864

I slept under the stars last night, and they were real nice. I love to look at them against the dark blue. They let a lot of light down on the ground and I could see things around me good. I think I will go for a swim this morning again before I eat.

July 30, 1864

It is so pretty here that I hate to think about going home. I like my house and all, but it is too quiet now and so empty. I will stay here a couple more days.

July 31, 1864

I wonder if I should have left a note in my house. If John stops by he might wonder where I am or get worried about me. I will have to explain to him that sometimes I just take off and go for long rides.

I think I will start for home this afternoon.

August 1, 1864

I got home last night just when it was getting dark. There was a light in my house, but I didn't see anybody around. I wondered if maybe it was John come to see me and staying to make sure I got home safe. I went to the barn with my horse and there were others in there too. There was a wagon sitting outside the barn and I looked at it close but couldn't tell whose it was. I looked at the horses again and decided I should be real careful going inside.

I stepped in the door and looked around real fast and my heart beat hard and I started to cry at what I saw.

Martha and Samuel were in my bed sleeping, and Kirk was sitting at that ol' sawbuck table reading a newspaper. When he saw me he came over fast and took my arm. It is a good thing he did too or I might have fallen down. He said that they had been lonesome for me, and he had to bring them to see me. He pointed at the children when he said it. I said I sure was glad because I missed them so much that it was hurting me. He said he understood how a person could feel that way. I asked him how long he could stay and he didn't answer me. He just asked if I was hungry and he got me something to drink while I waited for my supper. He sat beside me then, watching me eat. I didn't mind because I was so glad to have him there and it felt like a real house again. I asked him how long he been there and he told me two days. I said how sorry I was, and if I had known that he was coming I would have been home. He said that he hadn't known himself that he was coming until he did it, and he hoped I didn't mind.

Well, I finished eating and Kirk took my hand real light between his big ones and looked at it a minute and even ran his fingers over mine, and I thought I would die because of the feelings he made me feel then. He said he had something very important he needed to ask me and talk to me about. Then he spoke real fast, and I couldn't say anything until he was through. He asked if I would love his children forever, if I could take them and raise them as if they were mine. I nodded. He asked if I could care for them and love them always even after I had children of my own, and I nodded again. He then asked if there was any way that I might be able to take him and love him as well.

I told him YES, and I threw my hands around his neck and hugged him so close that he felt like he belonged there. I hugged him and told him that I already loved him and his children.

He pulled back from me, looked at me real serious, and asked, "Then you'll marry me?"

"I will!" I answered, and he smiled real big and kissed me.

We talked for a long time, and neither of us wanted to go to bed but we finally did. He went out on the porch and left me the floor in front of the stove.

August 2, 1864

I woke up early this morning—I hardly slept last night! How I love this world! How I love these children who are now sleeping beside me, and how I love Kirk White! I have never been happier in my life, and I know this is what God wants for me. I know it is what Ashley wants. Over and over in my heart I say, "Thank you God! And thank you Ashley for sharing your husband with me!"

I was granted the great honor this morning of telling little Martha and Samuel that I would be with them forever, and that I would never let them leave me. I told them that I was going to marry their father, and that we were going to have a beautiful life together and have more children for them to help me with. They are excited, but not any more than I am. I can barely even write these words while I think of my dreams and my new life that's now coming.

Now I look back on the pages I have written and I have to laugh and cry and wonder.

—From the journals of Cateline Fortier White

CHAPTER SIXTEEN

A NEW LIFE

August 5, 1864

We told the Pratts our news today, and I have never seen them happier. Those three women took my measurements and started a dress right then for me to be married in, and I know it will be perfect. I did not know such happiness existed before, and it is only to get better—I am sure—when I say my vows and have Kirk as my husband.

August 6, 1864

John came today to offer his congratulations. He shook Kirk's hand real firm and smiled at us both. He said he was real pleased, but that Kirk better take good care of me or he would see to it that Kirk wouldn't feel too good either. Kirk said John didn't need to worry and that he was welcome to come see us any time just to be sure. We laughed and John shared supper with us and played with the children until they fell asleep. He left us then and said he'd be at the wedding.

Kirk wrapped his arms around me and gave me a big hug and a quick kiss on the lips and then he hurried out of the house to sleep in the barn where he has set up a little room of his own. I stared at the door and wished I could hold him longer, but I knew our time would come.

August 7, 1864

I think that I won't have time to write again until after we are married—it is so busy and so fun to pack my things and to try on my dress.

Kirk is the best man I have ever met, and I am so very glad he asked me to be his wife. He is strong and handsome and a great father—I don't even have to wonder what kind of father he would be because I have seen him with his children and know already! He is good to me too and—well—I love him!

August 30, 1864

Kirk White and I were married on August 8, 1864! Now I am Mrs. Kirk White and I have never been more proud of my name. I still find it unbelievable that a man like Kirk would ask me to raise his children and be his wife! What a wonderful thing! Our wedding was perfect and our wedding night—well that will stay in my memory as perfect as it happened. I know without a doubt that this is the right thing and that Kirk loves me more than the world.

We spent the night at my little cabin on our wedding night and then we put my things in his wagon and moved to Kirk's. He sure has a fine place! I look around and can't believe it is mine—this home—this man and the children. God has blessed me!

August 8, 1888

I just read through my journal and believe it is time to name it—*My Spiritual Trail*—because that is what it was, and that is what it continues to be. Every time I read my scriptures, every time I hug my children I feel it and I know it is continuing. God has given me knowledge greater than I ever thought I could possess, and today the most incredible moment of my life has taken place. My six beautiful children joined Kirk and me as we knelt across the alter of the Manti Temple to be sealed together for eternity. And I cried to God in my mind—thank you, thank you! A greater gift I have never been given than the knowledge that now I will be with Kirk and our children forever.

Now I look back on the pages I have written and I have to laugh and cry and wonder. What a wonderful thing it is to have a record of my life and to let my children read it and get to know me better. And what a wonderful thing it is to grow!

My dearest Ashley—if you can hear me—and I know you can. I have changed my mind on so many things—so many teachings that confused me and made me wonder about the church make sense now. Ashley—how would it be for either of us if God did not allow us to have this husband?

ABOUT THE
AUTHOR

A native of Highland, Utah, Robyn Heirtzler grew up with a rich heritage of pioneer ancestry. That heritage has had a strong influence on the values and beliefs instilled in her throughout her life. That same heritage inspired her to begin writing in the historical genre.

Robyn has served in the Primary, Young Women, and scouting organizations in her various wards and currently serves as the Webelos den leader.

In addition to writing historical fiction, Robyn enjoys teaching others how to preserve their heritage in books of their own. She also enjoys history, photography, fishing, hiking, and boating with her family and friends. She has worked as a managing editor and staff writer for two weekly newspapers and has had articles published in various other publications.

Robyn resides in southern Utah with her husband, Dwayne, and their five children.

0 26575 79150 1